# Shawn Shook

# Memoir of a Derelict

A work of fiction

By Brooks Doherty

with Ellis Worth

PikeMag Books  -  St Paul, MN

*Shawn Shook: Memoir of a Derelict* is a PikeMag Book

www.pikemagbooks.com

PikeMag Books
P.O. Box 120666
Saint Paul, MN 55112


ISBN: 978-0-6152-0812-1


Chapters of *Shawn Shook: Memoir of a Derelict* have been published by Pike Magazine, an online arts space.

www.pikemag.com

For Tiffany and Ellis

*... which down their channels fret,*
*Even more than when I tripped lightly as they;*
*The innocent brightness of a new-born Day*
*Is lovely yet*

*-William Wordsworth*

# Chapter 1

PEOPLE ALONE are boring. It's their stories that are worthy of note. So if Elizabeth Bishop can get away with a poem about eight bodies (ashtray) and a full moon (gooseneck lamp) on her desk and get away with it, I should at least be allowed to do this.

## Just a Tad of That *Me* Mush

Books like these, I know are supposed to, or at least historically, include a series childhood anecdotes meant to delineate the current self. Maybe I was a virgin until I was 28. Maybe I stayed high from the first Bush through the next. Maybe my father was a priest or my mother a bodybuilder. Maybe I was kidnapped by the garbage man or sold to David Copperfield, who trained me to be his pedicurist. Maybe I had too many zits.

But none of this happened. (I did have zits: Not so many as to stand out as abnormal in junior high context; not so clear-complexioned as to be blessed.) My early childhood was pedestrian, pocked by baseball games, Legos, and loving dinners. I got laid in high school, but was neither suitably cute nor silver-tongued enough to be capable of full-blown promiscuity. I think I had three or five on-and-off girlfriends then, some of whom occasionally kissed me publicly in the lunchroom. Some of whom did not. Either way, nothing monumental.

My parents were divorced, but the split wasn't so messy as to be notable. I smoked pot occasionally, drank only at parties, ingested LSD two or three times.[1] Now I'm just on Jameson, lager, and Marlboros. Standard stuff.

Frankly, I didn't retain much information or experience from the age of 10 to that of 19. I stayed pat. Nothing pleased me greatly. Slightly more upset me. Frankly, very little of consequence has happened to me then or since. I have no idea why I have the right to write.

Even if I am without such authorization, I do have permission to read. And mimesis is just a hop and a skip from there. So there.

I DON'T remember when I began reading but I remember why. Of course, my mom read to me before I could make choices. But then, children are not intelligent enough to be who they are. There are no three-year-old vegetarians, no iconoclastic sucklings. Toddlers don't hear a reading of *Green Eggs & Ham* and think, "A tad hackneyed, yet flavorful." They don't do that because they're not smart.

And that has nothing to do with why I read books.

My ninth grade English lit instructor, Ms. Kelly, made us read three novels over our fourteen weeks: *The Grapes of Wrath*, *A Choice of Weapons*, and *This Side of Paradise*. No attention was paid to the first two but I was bewildered by the latter. My chest and throat constricted at the thought of being Ivy League. At the time, I assumed this physical reaction was a symptom of delight. Now, older, I am unsure. That aside, in reading *This Side*, I began jotting down every unusual mention I fell over: What is

---

[1] During one trip on a friend's brother's uncut acid, I broke my ankle in a fall off the roof of a warming house. I had climbed it trying to touch the moon. While a mildly interesting story (I just told you all I know) it certainly was not a governing experience. It has nothing to do with why I write.

"Claire de Lune"? What language is this *Et je pleure* shit? What do spires have to do with gargoyles?

"Dad? What do spires have to do with gargoyles?"

My father was building a drink. "Gs & Ts bring Zs," he always said.

Dad, balding and slender with his customary yellow-tee-and-boxers uniform of the evening, never stirred. He twirled his spirits with his mixers, when they were present, clacking ice against sides of his soaring plastic cup. "Spires and gargoyles? Nothing. Why?"

"I read it in a book: 'Spires and Gargoyles.' What's a spire?"

"It's like those staircases that twirl up, like your aunt's. Who cares? Spires." My father trailed off with his sip. His hairy earlobes sunk to the earth as his neck bent back to drink. I shot back.

"What's *ett juh plurry?*"

"What? Ask your mother," he crunched ice and turned his attention back to the open jar.

"What's fellatio?"

To this, my dad snickered and coughed once with a smile, leaning into the bottle.

Turning back to me encouragingly, dad tutored: "You're dreamin'. Beat it."

So I did. And that's why I started reading.


BEING something of an information literacy genius (and a book mime), I not only found answers to all my Fitzgerald questions independently, but pursued them as experiences, some earlier than others. I learned French; if Fitzgerald mentioned Schopenhauer, I read him; I tried desperately to be puzzled and depressed by *Portrait of the Artist as Young Man*, too; and nebulous lustre was born.

I created a slight Fitzgerald-centered org chart that I may or may not still have to this day. I know I took it with me to college. It was my bookmark.

The greatest lesson I learned in my seven years at the University of Minnesota is that it is much easier – and sometimes more beneficial – to stare at something than to read it. Words are abstract. Images are not. Am I not closer to reality and thus the truth if I watch television or the inside of my eyelids instead of reading that which was assigned? I believe so. My instructors and the federal government, which provided the bulk of my loans, did not. Nonetheless, I gazed my way through college – occasionally reading, but mostly blending in as one of our campus's thirty-two thousand *flâneurs*. The difference was: Others experienced. I just walked.

Reading always cast me intro trouble. Gazing rarely did. There was one occasion when a young exchange student[2] approached me in the campus noodle shop and asked, attempting to gain friends, what I was reading. (I, in fact, was skimming three E.M Forster novels bound together, *reading* nothing.) Seven seconds of silence and an absence of eye contact followed his initial inquiry. So he spoke up again:

"My, that's a thick book. You must be studying looooo."

I responded. Not out of bonhomie but confusion. "What? Studying what?"

"Looooo."

"I'm sorry. I'm not following. I'm reading Forster. And what is Looooo?"

"You know, looooo. You read big looooo books and you become a solicitor."

---

[2] From Britain, I now infer.

"A what? I assure you, I've no aspirations of…. I'm an English major and this is… What are you on?"

"Forget it. You just… I just got accepted to the U's Looooo School. I thought that… Forget it."

And he walked away. I sucked up a noodle, placed my Fitzgerald org chart between pages twelve and thirteen and left.

Law.

My idiocy arrived as an epiphany as I set first foot on sidewalk. Was I studying Law. Fuck. No.

College was more than a half-decade-long succession of such crossed wires and awkward communication. I left the dorms on weekends to drink with my high school friends. They got me. Momentarily. Then back to school on Monday. And back home. And again. For six years.

I took part in commencement after five. But upon opening the diploma shell handed to me on stage, I read a jagged piece of cardboard whose message read something like, "You're not commencing a thing."

It was true I hadn't yet submitted my senior thesis[3], but still.

After another year of revising and gazing at revisions, I was given my walking paper. That is, the shiny cardboard segment which reads, in not so many words, "You're done. Now get." As I ambled off campus and into adulthood, the university, like a spurned lover, stood at the third floor window of my old dorm room, pissed, slinging hunks of my edification at my head and neck.

---

[3] Entitled "Prufrock and Roll: How Eliot's Masterpiece Gave Birth to America's Music"

I now know that no one can take your education away from you; but many will borrow it, fold it up like a perfect little paper airplane, and hurl its pointy end at your eyes.

AND SCHOOL taught me nothing. It only gave me the knowledge to validate the suspicions I have had since birth.

THOSE WHO say English majors are limp couldn't be more wrong.[4] Try lifting forty thousand hardcover books in one afternoon; appraise crippling pains that shoot through my twisting knees – the crouching, the sore forearms, and the sweat leaping from strands of hair onto fresh copies of *Impossible Vacation* and infinitesimal cuts on the palm of my hand. Try it. Then see if you think I'm soft.

The evening after my first day on the bookstore job, about two years ago, I couldn't eat; six splinters were sunk into my thumbs and index fingers, the result of hurling pallets into a dumpster. The little logs would neither allow me to grasp utensils nor handle finger food without feeling as if Flames of Hell were licking artificial butter off my hands.

It's tough work. Books are heavy. Being a stock boy at a boxy leviathan book retailer is very blue collar, so proletarian. So Arturo Bandini in the fish cannery.

That said, however, I am fed free coffee each morning; I receive a ten percent employee discount, and – this is my personal pleasure – the new blue carpet in the

---

[4] Grammar rules stipulate that all single syllable words require the addition of *-er* in the comparative; the exceptions—for reasons that must be absolutely intriguing—are *right*, *wrong*, and *real*. Wronger means: One who does wrong.

children's section smells absolutely intoxicating. But this job, like its myriad perks, is but fleeting.

Today and since those days of youthful literary exploration, furtively, I have dreamt of being a legendary (and hermetic!) *homme de lettres*: Beckettian in both demeanor and legacy[5]: Anaemic sales with an obese presence on postgraduate syllabi. But that will be then; today, my English Literature degree has earned me a nine-dollar-an-hour gig at the world's third largest bookseller. "We" recently opened a thirty-five-thousand square foot, three-floor lair at the suburban mall just down the street from my apartment. I'm not allowed overtime and "we" have neither medical nor dental benefits until I'm considered a permanent employee. Exactly when that day will come I am unsure, but today, I do get that sweet concession on books and stationary.

I don't read much anymore. I've been trying to finish *The Great Gatsby* for about a month. Most of my leisure reading takes place during lunch breaks. Each day, my supervisor Char – a large, nondescript woman of forty-five with product-free, pony-tailed hair and Sammy Davis, Junioresque glasses – places a bright yellow sticker on my copy of *Gatsby* as a measure to ensure it – a 1954 Charles Scribner's Sons edition with yellowed pages and a chewed-up cover upon which is stamped COOPER HIGH SCHOOL MEDIA CENTER – truly belongs to me and has not been pinched from the fiction section. Our brief conversations during these transactions invariably end with one party cussing out the other.

---

[5] I once had a vision that goes like this: a critic asks me what my latest short story means. *"Means?"* I reply, "Don't ask me what it *means*. It's an object. Nothing more." There's his column right there. I think that was a vision.

The conclusion of each shift requires me to punch out and request that Char remove that day's decal and, after my bag is searched thoroughly for purloined book lamps and/or our very popular beeswax lip gloss, I am praised for my day's work.

"Good work today, Shawn. See you tomorrow."

"Fuck off immediately, Char."

So many theft-protection labels have been placed on my book that it has grown sticky. But things could be worse. It's not like I'm breaking rocks. I'm not swinging metal into more metal. I couldn't. I'm the Henry Miller at the dead end of a John Henry lineage.

As a teenager, my grandfather worked as a gas attendant for a weekly wage of twenty eight cents. In his early twenties, Papa worked eighteen hours a day on the railroad. By the time he was thirty, he had built a successful trucking company. Near the end of his life, Papa's second entrepreneurial undertaking, a painting business, routinely topped ten million dollars in annual sales. He sired ten children, who in turn cranked out 26 grandchildren. He died busy and, as Dr. Phil would say, successful.

I am staring thirty in the face and the most daunting accomplishment listed on my CV is the completion of *Ulysses* and *À la recherche du temps perdu* – sans annotated guides. These triumphs, however, were not enough for Char to place me anywhere near the fiction section.[6] I routinely stock seven-page (very thick, cardboard pages often adorned with tufts of cotton, ribbon, and those plastic googly eyes) books on pastel

---

[6] She may have sensed that the largest undertaking on my CV was also its largest lie. Like most English majors, I have yet to finish *Ulysses* (I simply flinched when asked about Molly Bloom's soliloquy during my interview) and hated the only volume of Proust I have ever touched. I'd sooner drink cat piss than read about self-destructive and unemployed *belle époque* French aristocrats.

shelves in the children's section. Occasionally, I lead our monthly Story Time Event, during which I, too, am required to wear ribbons and googly eyes.

Countless nights I have lain awake attempting to reassemble my employers' logic in determining my section placement, considering my professed literary acumen. So far, all I have come up with is this: Proust is purple; the shelves in the children's section are purple; let's stick him there.

Neither of my parents have a college education. Both motivated by a combination of intrinsic ardor and extrinsic drink, they have lives and vocations over which I could drool (and have literally done so on select Friday nights). My mother runs my late Papa's company. Though she doesn't earn enough for the both of us, I envy her sense of family tradition and her firm position within ours.

Our family mythos is comprised only of the strongest bits of the Sanos[7] lineage. Without a *real* job I do not feature in this. (Also, I missed eight or nine family reunions during the 1990s for disparate reasons ranging from clinical depression to leaking transmission to hangover.) Neither my cousin Josh nor his ideals feature in this mythology either. They had when he was on tract to receive his MBA at the age of twenty, but at the age of twenty-two Josh was incarcerated for snapping the necks of a dozen puppies. My great aunt Sis is only included in our Sanos family legend during lubricated talks at family events she does not attend. Sis has the reputation of an angel when she's not around. She has what I believe to be a mild form of either Asperger Syndrome or Alzheimer's disease, although no such diagnosis has, to the family's knowledge, been made.

---

[7] Sanos is my mother's maiden name. My surname, from my father's side, is Shook. My first name is Shawn.

My uncle Phil is the foundation of the family ideal despite his continuing accusations that I am a homosexual. For me, his public indictments are particularly flustering considering Phil was an usher at my wedding[8] only three years ago. If I were given the task of constructing the Sanos clan's mythos, Phil would be dislodged and treated like Josh's dogs.

Unfortunately, my charge lies elsewhere: Customer service. I employ the knowledge gained at university to hawk lattes and ensure the edges of the new Ann Coulter book are properly aligned with those of the display table. Whatever.

I love my patrons, several of whom I consider friends. Others I consider annoying. Still others I consider abducting and disemboweling.

Allow me now to supply you with my choicest bookstore[9] anecdotes.

LAST summer, an attractive young brunette entered the store and browsed my region. Per store policy, I greeted her after she had come within ten feet of my person[10] and asked if she needed assistance. She with troubled brown eyes, perfectly painted lips, and freshly washed sweat pants responded that she was looking for a gift for her roommate who had read "like, every book on the planet." This roommate's favorite authors, I was told, were Wilde and James. I suggested several titles from these authors, including *De Profundis, The Importance of Being Earnest,* and *What Maisie Knew*, in the hopes that I would simultaneously impress this casually-dressed creature with my knowledge of

---

[8] To a woman.

[9] I refrain from sharing with you the name of my employer due to fear of litigation. But here is a hint: its name starts with the eleventh letter of the alphabet. I swear to you, no other information will be withheld through the balance of this text.

[10] Not infrequently I scamper away from unattractive customers or those whom I have seen in the science fiction section so as to keep them outside my ten foot bubble. It's like getting paid for playing tag.

literature and achieve my quota of three referrals per customer contact. If all went accordingly, My Sweet Consumer would soon walk through our automatic doors, beepless, with my phone number, a few books, and an add-on: Maybe an electronic gift card or a cube of spiced pumpkin cake.

Indeed, she was impressed with my bookish erudition and asked:

"How do you know all these books?"

"I was an English Lit major in college."

"Oh, my God! Me too! English is my strongness."

Silence.

"Clearly," I mumbled.

"I'm sorry?"

"As am I. Did you know all our coffee is fair trade?"

She flirted with me for sad eternity. My dream dissolved, I passed her off to another bookseller who later told me the girl left our store with a five-dollar birthday card for her roommate and seven-dollar mocha for herself.


IN ANOTHER instance, an older woman who had passed within ten feet announced that her son, who was of mixed race, had recently developed a vehement hatred for not only white civilization ("the White Power Structure" she said he had called it) but also for the white blood within his body.

"Do you happen to sell anything that could teach my son about the pleasures and benefits of being white?

Silence.

How to handle this? Three referrals? Jump back quickly so as to create more than ten feet of space?

After making uninterrupted and blinkless eye contact for at least thirty seconds with this woman, I composed myself and replied:

"You may want to consider Edie Brickell's new greatest hits album entitled *Cassingle*, which was just released Tuesday. All the Caucasians are buying it. And in our multi-media department you will find DVD boxed sets of *Friends*. Follow me. I'll walk you over."

I was perilously close to, as a third referral, suggesting she and her son start a grassroots campaign opposing Channel Seven's habit of broadcasting syndicated reruns of *A Different World* Monday mornings at 11:00. But there's no way I could have kept a straight face.

After enjoying a slice of cheesecake and a medium coffee (black), the white woman left our store with a thirty-eight-dollar copy of *The Price of the Ticket* by James Baldwin. I told her it was a non-fiction book about suburban transportation issues.

Those are just two of my many bookstore tales. But enough shop talk. Let's discuss me.

## More Me, Incongruously

SHOOK is an American corruption of the clan name of my Irish ancestors: Sioc, (pronounced *shuk*) which is Irish Gaelic for *frost*. My Christian name, Shawn, too, is a defilement of the Irish *Seán*, which is the equivalent of the English-language name John, one of whose numerous possible nicknames is Jack.

My parents named me Jack Frost, the character from (absurdly) Viking folklore who personifies frigidity. He is also the namesake of the slasher movie franchise whose films feature a psychotic snowman murdering women and children with wintry weaponries.[11] If I can recall correctly, in one scene, Jack Frost coaxes a young boy into sticking his tongue onto an ice-covered metal pole before mutilating him, leaving a severed head stuck to the icy post.

I used to read voraciously the works of Irish writers with noble names like O'Connor, O'Brien, Corkery, O'Casey, Kavanagh, Yeats, Beckett, and Behan. But I am Jack Frost. And Shawn Shook.

Like most English majors, my heroes are dead. My greatest inspiration is my deceased great uncle, Edward Sanos.[12] He died, thirteen years before my birth, too young, of a heart attack. My grandmother told me that Edward, her brother, frequently flirted with death by hopping trains from Minnesota to Colorado (and back again), an attorney traversing The Great Plains in the company of hobos and mice. On more than one occasion, Grandma said, Edward was very nearly murdered by one of his human rail companions. He once witnessed a novice train-hopper shot to death for not relinquishing his pocket watch to a frequent traveler who took it upon himself to be the box car's toll collector. "Lead poisoning," Grandma called this manner of death. I never knew if her *lead* referred to the watch or the bullet.

Great Uncle contributed regularly to *Reader's Digest*, graduated law school at the age of nineteen[13], and – according to legend – would consistently perplex and offend his

---

[11] Snowballs, icicles, freshly sharpened figure skates, et cetera.
[12] A writer whose pen name was Ellis Worth.
[13] Pointlessly, it seems, since Minnesota law at the time prohibited anyone under the age of twenty-one from practicing law.

relatives with his vast vocabulary: They were perplexed because they didn't understand what Edward was saying; they were offended because they knew that these utterances were his preferred means of their disparagement. For me, words are a way to live outside myself. For Edward, I gather, they were a means of digging into others. That's all I know.

I have never read Edward's bludgeoning words, but I may get that chance tonight.[14] His magazine articles are out of print. His manuscripts have disappeared, grandma told me. But the morning that finds me writing these words to you greeted me with a phone call. Aunt Sis rang, shaking me out of a chemical slumber, to tell me that she had obtained three short stories believed to have been written by Ellis Worth. I asked her where and how she came about them. She responded with the *click* and *hooogh* of a freshly lit cigarette.

That's my special occasion, the *vis major* that prompted me to dig a notebook out of my college backpack and write. I promise you the pages of this memoir heretofore were not intended to, as most memoirs do, secure your sympathy for my painfully typical life through solipsistic jottings. And henceforth, I will do my best to shelter you from the pitiful details of my sloth, my self-indulgence, my silent pride, and my sad airs. I decided to start writing after receiving Sis's phone call. I decided to write not for myself, but for an event, for the only member of my family to whose éclat I can relate. The grand narratives of Life and Death and America and Communism and Christ and Food and Water and Words and Society are dead now. So instead of delving into the next logical alternative (Me), I will identify my aunt's phone call as an arbitrary genesis and go on. Because that's all I have to offer.

---

[14] *Tonight* meaning the night on which I write these words. Throughout this memoir, I shall narrate from various dates, times, geographic locations, and planes of existence. There will be other tonights I will write about that will not be *tonight*. Please keep up.

I will hide from you, but I will not lie. I have haphazardly dashed through my feeble and few childhood memories, relative bios, professional endeavors, and personal orthographical history because they are tedious bits of fact and/or truth. In short, they are unimportant relative to the stories.

The words above were not memoirs or *memoire* or memory or *smarati* or *memoria*. Just a bowlful of clips, starts, and stops. The rest may construct my grand bricolage.

## The Stories

SIS IS likely lying about the manuscripts' existence in order to lure me onto her couch so she can throw beer cans at my chest. Aunt Sis, in my opinion, can never again be fully trusted after telling the family during the highball toast at her seventieth birthday celebration that she was pregnant and planned to dispose of the fetus.

Sis is one of two breathing relatives with whom I don't mind spending time. Despite familial speculation, I don't think she is diseased. I just think she doesn't *care*: She doesn't care enough to remember details about her nieces' and nephews' birthdays or baptisms, and doesn't care enough to spare anyone's feelings. She may or may not have a soft spot for me, however. I commonly visit her as I will tonight,[15] traveling by city bus to her home after my demoralizing bag check and sticker removal at the bookstore.

"TEA, BABY?"

"No, Auntie Sis. I'm tead out. Beer?"

---

[15] These words, I shakily write en route.

"But you're driving, you lush," she scolded, lurching over the counter with both hands bustling like those of a crocheter.

"No, I'm riding. I took the bus. I don't have a car, remember?"

"No."

Sis, wearing an enormous men's dress shirt and leopard Zubaz, flung a beer at me from the kitchen to the living room couch—a distance of about fifteen feet. The can thudded against my sternum. I popped it seconds later, slurping suds as I anticipated getting my now bubbled paws on Edward's manuscripts. My hopes were not utterly up, though.

As I performed this beer maintenance, my anxiety caused the clutter of Aunt Sis's home to close in on me. I visit often, as mentioned, but until this night had never noticed the prodigious amount of detritus she employs as decorative filler. Her tiny living room was filled with so many tiny lamps, lacy dolls, and talking stuffed animals—Teddy Ruxpin, Tickle Me Elmo, and the rest. This collection is *not* one of my aunt's hobbies[16] but rather an eccentricity forced upon her by my relatives and me.

A cousin once, long ago, without an idea of what to buy a woman who had (almost literally) everything (crammed into her diminutive apartment), gave her one of these verbose monsters as a gift. Other relatives, similarly lacking inspiration, followed suit. Now, thanks to us – for I, too, contributed to this convoy with a Little Mermaid Shimmering Ariel (the one that swears) – Aunt Sis is known as the crazy woman with the loud toys.

My favorite piece of her tchotchke is a brown glass whale, half full of old wine that today must have the consistency of margarine. Sis says she and her late husband

---

[16] To wit, she had none.

were given the "bottle" in 1968 as an anniversary gift. She claims the whale is half empty because the cork (in the mammal's mouth) has dried, allowing water to evaporate. She swears she has never taken the beast for a sip. I believe her.

Although I have no recollection of imbibing its sweet innards, I cannot say for certain that I have not.

Aunt Sis's entertainment center is much too large for her living room. It nearly reaches the low ceiling[17] and juts out at least four feet from the wall, just to the left of the main entrance from the perspective of the deep red, botanical-patterned divan on which I now sit. This Ikea-manufactured antipersonnel trap, resembling a particleboard outhouse, is responsible for at least seven forehead scars among my relatives of which I am aware, mostly given to deserving children who, hopped up on soda and cookies, ran wildly and took too hard a right turn from the kitchen into the living room. The carpet surrounding the entertainment center is noticeably stained with so many bloods similar to that which courses through my veins.[18] But, I swear, none of it has ever been mine.

"How's your new job?" Sis shouted from somewhere.

"It's terrible, but a man's gotta eat."

"That's the rumor," Sis spouted in cliché as she is wont to do. She, now easily into her eighth decade, looked younger somehow than she did last week. Still very grey, but vivid. The skin on her hands, flailing about with smoke trailing her fingers as she bounced into the living room, was taut in a youthful, not bloated, way. Despite this external glow, her lungs were not fairing well.

---

[17] The whale sits atop this box. The creature's fin—yes, the blower gave it an anatomically incorrect *fin*—scrapes her ceiling.

[18] And maybe a splash of whale wine?

Sis sighed as she sank into the sofa,[19] her huge shirt inflating like a parachute. "What brings you tonight?"

I wasn't sure.

"Unsure. I think I need that gold mining book of yours. That *Westward Ho!* or whatever."

"Shit. I just sat down. Now you want me to bring out boxes."

"Sorry, Sis, but you know how I'm hungry for history," I responded without conviction.

"Hungry for free drink, more like it. I thought your little degree was in books. Not history. Why do you care."

This final utterance was more of a statement than a question, so I didn't respond. The numerous song birds – linnets and bowers – caged throughout the room had exploded in chirps just as Auntie spoke. So I wasn't sure of exactly what she had said.

"Just get the box," I sipped from my can.

She sipped, "Never tell me what to do. I brought you into this world and I *will* take you out."

"You're not my mother, *Auntie*. You're my Aunt, Sis."

"Well, I was in the delivery room. I could have ended you then. Maybe should have."

"Whatever. Bring out the box, lady."

---

[19] The great Minnesota writer Tim O'Brien once attempted to shock an audience of undergraduates (of which I was part) away from alliteration with the sentence: "The red, rollicking river of his tongue rubbed me the wrong way." Of course I would never go that far. I consider myself a centrist when it comes to phoneme-level rhetorical schemes.

"All right," she ejaculated as she forced her fat body off the furniture with her left hand, her right hand still clutching a beer can.

As she waddled out through the kitchen to the basement, I gazed back at that goddamned booze whale. I wanted a swig. Would I be the first? Would the cork crumble in my palm? I would certainly be caught. Auntie would certainly kill me. But, oh! How drunk I would become! How warm I would become, inebriated with whale wine as I flipped through *Westward Ho!* and possibly the works of my great uncle, knowing something that only I knew: I had cracked the whale and drunk his concentrated soul, and by the time Sis would discover the drink level down, if ever, she would have no clue as to whom was the culprit. She probably would not care. Dozens, maybe more, have read *Westward Ho!*. But no one has ever reached inside the whale. Jonas the Stock Boy. Jonas the Pillager. Jonas the Only. Should I do it?

I will do it.

"Here's your box."

She's back. You win this round, whale.

Sis's Sanos Family Box contained reams of copies of birth and death certificates that my aunt had painstakingly and very expensively collected from county courthouses throughout Minnesota. In addition, it contained books published by the state historical societies that featured the names of my forefathers: Books dealing in matters ranging from gold-digging to railroading, from architecture to the purported life of Saint Patrick.[20]

---

[20] Our family has been accused of kidnapping Patrick from England and bringing him to Ireland, where, famously, he proselytized and converted the druids, helping to spread Christianity throughout western Europe. He also inspired dozens of generations of youth worldwide to drink to violent excess each March 17, which my friends and I now refer to as Amateur Night.

"Your other Auntie Bett just sent me some things you might want to see. She had three short stories that Edward wrote, unpublished.[21] They're in the box."

It was true. Maybe.

Silence.

I dug through the contents of the box that originally contained a microwave oven. Books. Books. Manila folders. Binders from the Goodhue County Historical Society. Books.

Shhhhh. Here they are.

"I should have drunk that whale."

Birds chirped.

"I'm sorry?"

"As am I."

---

[21] Lazy people believe, a smart man once said, that stories require no justification; they just are. I am lazy and this is my conviction.

Tim O'Brien's first novel was entitled *Timmy of the Little League*. He wrote it in one ninety minute setting at the Nobles County Library in Worthington, Minnesota, in (probably, he says) the summer of 1958. O'Brien, after a particularly horrendous day playing shortstop for his Little League team, trudged dustily to the library, where he found a book entitled *Larry of the Little League* (O'Brien once told a University of Minnesota audience, "This kid Larry could do everything I couldn't do: he could field, hit, run, and throw. I finished the book, marched over to the librarian, asked for a pad of paper and a pen, which she gave to me, went back to my desk, and over the course of the next hour and a half—at age nine, possibly ten—composed the first novel of my life, or what I thought of as a novel. The title was *Timmy of the Little League*, essentially a rip-off of Larry."). Timmy's Worthington Ben Franklin team beat Edina in the state Little League championship game and Taiwan in the Little League World Series championship game in Williamsport, Pennsylvania by a score of eighty to nothing. In both games, Timmy got the game-winning hit. O'Brien claims his parents still have a copy of *Timmy of the Little League* ("this aborted effort," he calls it). I would love to read it, if for no other reason to see how one delivers a game-winning hit in a game whose final score is eighty to zip.

Now this is the part I hate. The *Timmy of the Little League* story is so entrenched in my mind, soul, kidneys, scalp, stomach, and being that I could recite it and the rest of O'Brien's hour-long lecture nearly verbatim. If I were to recite the entire speech from memory, any crowd would regard my act as that of a genius. However, if I were to write it down from memory, make copies, and distribute the copies to that same crowd, my act would be regarded as criminal. So, in order to avoid any legal stumbles, it is with saliva-souring dismay that I inform you the above information was both gleaned and quoted directly from Tim O'Brien's *Writing Vietnam* presidential lecture on 21 April 1999. I was in the audience that night and I regard the lecture as mine. Alas, however, it is not.

The sheets of paper on which the three stories were typed were still white, if thinning. Across each page the word "COPY" was splashed diagonally from the lower left toward the upper right in three-inch letters.

The three stories were entitled "Revolution in the Rain", "The Path", and "School for Scoundrels". I felt an obsessive need to be alone with the works of Ellis Worth, so I surreptitiously tucked the fragile manuscripts into my jacket as I flipped, ostensibly occupied, through *Westward Ho!*. She won't miss them. And they are mine more than anyone else's. I took in the dregs of my beer and fled for my bus, so anxious to be alone that I stubbed my toe on the entertainment center just as I informed Sis that I had left the iron plugged in.[22] Shoulders down, I skipped through the frozen December air, bruised, maybe[23], but never bleeding.


TEN MINUTES at a bus stop in a Minnesota winter is a godforsaken eternity, especially when you are plump with unread stories. Ice had begun to develop on my eyelashes. My earlobes were numb. My once-aching toe and the other nine were by now numb and curled. My facial hair had hardened to a cluster of sewing needles.

To offset this discomfort, I forced myself to imagine being submerged: Sliding down porcelain into a warm bath, letting hot bubbles pour from my nose and mouth, eyes open and burning. I see the movement of my toes from underwater, and those I recognize only due to the understanding that I am wiggling them. I can feel my hair drifting like seaweed. My muscles had begun to melt when the bus tires crunched to a halt.

---

[22] Rather than, "...I informed Sis that in I had left the iron plugged."
[23] I never did pull off my sock to look.

# Chapter 2

*"Clearly he did not care about creating a unified allegory or a coherent story. The images of the Black Paintings do not cohere, or not in that way. One cannot even be sure of the apparent links between them."*       *-Robert Hughes*

## Revolution in the Rain

IF NOTHING had happened at all, this would have been an unusual Saturday – one set aside for the extraordinary. A real rainy spell in Colorado is decidedly rare, but on this occasion rain had fallen intermittently all day Friday and through the night. Moreover, every indication pointed to more of the same on this first Saturday in June – that is, raining, stopping, starting over again, with only the overcast remaining constant. Mr. Dana Duckwald would visit his sons as always on Saturday, but, as will be seen, the two of them would rival the weatherman in – in – well, call it caprice.

Since Mr. Duckwald's last visit the preceding week, his elder son, Abbott, had had his seventeenth birthday. As a gift from his mother, the boy had received what he long had asked for and what the father had long opposed: a .22 automatic rifle. Abbott had found a pretext, even, on Thursday evening, for stopping by his father's home with the gun still in the box and for remarking that he had been out target practicing with Biff Madden and Sterling Jones, and, now, would Dad drive him home. Dana said certainly he would but he did not inspect the gun or ask to see it. He did unbend enough, as they were driving along, to say: "You know I've never wanted you to have a gun: and you know why. But now that you have one, I hope you enjoy it and have good luck with it."

Abbot said, "I know, Dad... If anyone ever tries to break into the house at night, I'll probably take the gun by the barrel and hit the guy over the head with the stock!"

"Not a bad idea, at that," Mr. Duckwald replied. "I always used to say, in the war, that if a German suddenly popped his head over a rock at me, I'd throw my pistol at him... I wouldn't, I suppose, but I used to say that."

"I'm glad you didn't turn that hand-made shoulder-holster in to the Army, Dad... I've got that in my dresser, you know..."

That conversation had been on a warm, summery, Thursday evening: and now here it was a cool, rainy, Saturday morning... Marzda, the ex-wife, the mother of the boys, would be away from home all day, as usual, but Mr. Duckwald never felt comfortable spending any length of time in her house, and he and his sons had become habituated in ten years of visits to active outdoor pursuits: baseball, tennis, skating, skiing and so forth.

The younger son, Clive, met his father with, "Scotty Loomis and I are going hunting magpies... Can I?"

"Here are some rolls I got at the bakery on the way. Would you like some?... I'm afraid it's too wet for that sort of thing, Clive... You'd get your shoes and pants all wet... Where's Abbott?"

"He's still in bed. He'll want to sleep late. Don't waken him."

At this point, Abbott put in an appearance on the stairway. He was sleepy-eyed, and pajama-clad, but evidently hungry. He helped himself to a roll and went for a glass of milk.

"How'd you guys like a trip along Phantom Canyon today?"

*Here's my stop.*

# Lares and Penates

I LIVE on the third floor of a square apartment complex – Brighton Green Park – in the northern suburbs of Saint Paul. Fortunately, in arctic weather like this, my door is just a treacherous, unshoveled walkway and an obtrusive snow bank away from the bus stop. No elevator. I fly up the stinking staircase and let myself in room 305.

Crooked stacks of books would make my already minuscule apartment appear smaller to strangers, if such types were allowed in. There is no method to the literary litter – no alphabetizing, no genre sectioning, no attention paid to ISBN. The column nearest my couch is comprised of: *Crossing California, The Breaking of Nations, Sixteen Short Novels, Goya, Rats in the Grain, Fidel: A Critical Portrait, A Million Little Pieces, The Wretched of the Earth, The Cash Nexus, The Complete Works of Lewis Carroll, Irish in Minnesota, The Book of I Ching, The Autobiography of Malcolm X, The C.G. Jung Reader, and Dry.* On the floor near my father's plastic yellow ashtray rests *Sa biographie, les fresques, les toiles, les tapisseries, les eaux-fortes.*

If one were to inspect the pages of my books – no one ever has – s/he would find a variety of makeshift bookmarks[24] fitted between, on average, the twelfth and thirteenth page of each. I may be wrong in saying the following, but likely I am not: I don't believe I've finished reading a book since I was thirteen. Candidly, I rarely get past the first chapter of anything not assigned to me by a professor.

I have, however, consumed much of the latest printing of the Oxford English Dictionary[25], though, admittedly, I have committed little of it to memory. My apartment –

---

[24] Mostly sundry business cards, scrap papers, yarn, fancy laminated cardboard bits featuring Albert Einstein stolen from my place of employment, and the occasional snapped chow mein noodle.
[25] Retailing for over $895, and therefore stolen from the stock room.

nay! – my existence is a vortex of language. I spend much of my leisure time reading initial pages of books, discovering unfamiliar words[26], searching for their definitions in the OED which, sadly, leads me only to more unfamiliar words. I customarily end my literary voyage there.

Making up the several short stacks on my so-called kitchen table: *The Te of Piglet, Milk in My Coffee, Tropic of Capricorn, In the Lake of the Woods, An Introduction to Symbolic Logic, The Communist Manifesto, The Edmund Burke Reader, An Giall, The Rosicrucian Cosmo Conception, The Black Flag of Anarchy,* and *Spanish for Mastery: Bienvenidos,* to name most.

My favorite possession surveys the living room and its piles of tomes from above and behind my couch: It is a large framed poster of Beckett smoking a cigarette. Superimposed over the collar of his turtleneck is his quote:

*What Matter Who Speaks?*

This portrait, coupled with a degrading day of work, always makes me want to smoke. Ergo, I do. And drink. And Sam reads over my shoulder:


…MR. DUCKWALD asked. "It's too wet for almost everything else… This afternoon, if it's still raining, we can take in a movie. *Cimarron* is at the Rivoli."

"Gup and I planned to do some target-practising," Abbott replied abruptly. The Guptills were next-door neighbors and their only son was about Abbott's age.

Clive said, "Oh, you are? Can I go, too? Can I go with you?" He was two years younger than Abbott, and the latter sometimes would discover, to Clive's detriment, what

---

[26] One of the OED's many definitions of *word* is: as opposed to action.

a whale of a difference a few years make. This time, Abbott did not reply, but his silence was assenting.

Father Duckwald made no comment. He himself had discovered how revocable and tentative are the plans of youth – especially if not opposed dictatorially.

Clive went to the phone. "Hi, Scotty?! Say, I guess I can't go after magpies with you, after all... My brother's got a new gun, you know, a honey with synchronized action, and he's asked me to go target-practising with him..."[27]

"Watch him invite him to go with us," Abbott grumbled to his father. He rose from the table.

"Where you going?" Mr. Duckwald asked.

"Back to bed till Gup's ready. He said he'd call me as soon as he got up."

Clive finally finished talking with Scotty without urging his friend to join his brother's expedition. He right away spied that the rainfall had ceased for the time being. He made a bee-line for his room and returned with a baseball, mitt and glove.

"Come on, Dad," he boomed. "Let's toss the old apple around."

"It's too wet," the father said. "We'll get the cover soaked."

"No, we won't. We won't drop it."

"We surely will. We always drop it," the father said, but he accepted the mitt the son thrust upon him and followed Clive out the door and onto the driveway. There they

---

[27] Walter Pater believed that music was the most evolved of all art, and that "all art aspires to the condition of music." Anyone who has seen Prince perform likely agrees. We routinely see him (Prince, not Pater) merge songs seamlessly: From "7" into "Come Together", from "Crazy" into "Bop Gun" into "Let's Pretend We're Married" as if they were compounds made elements through a common and enlightened engineer. It's either an elevated literary sensitivity or ADHD, but I too am able to mentally weave texts (from the Latin *texere*) through one another. For example, after reading the denoted Ellis Worth passage above, I am reminded of this: "His eyes grew dim; he drew near it, he looked around for a chair—the chair sprang forward and placed itself under him—and he sat down in front of the portrait. He waved his hand, and all retired on their tiptoes, leaving the great man to himself and his feelings. (Tolstoy, Leo, War and Peace (1960). New York: International Collectors Library. p. 463)

stood, the two of them, throwing the ball back and forth easily, but with all the motions, contortions and gyrations of a big-league battery in action and with such a look of complete satisfaction on their faces as to suggest that this sport could go on all day – or forever. Then, a sudden shower sent them scurrying for the porch.

Father Duckwald went inside. "Get up Abbott," he called. We're going up to the Pass for lunch."

Abbott came downstairs as promptly as if he had been dressed and waiting for that very summons. He went to the phone and dialed. "Hoi, Gup?  I guess we'll have to call off that shooting. It'll be pretty moist up there… Yeah, OK."  He hung up.

He held out his hand to his father. Mr. Duckwald put the car keys in his son's hand and all three headed for the car. Clive got the back seat. He was silent. So was Abbott: even more so—to the point of being sullen and morose. All the way up the Pass and all through the lunch at Durban's summer-season restaurant, Mr. Duckwald labored to strike a spark of interest in his sons. They were like wet flints, but worse. It seemed that each one's hand was raised against the other, against him, against the world. Everyone, their attitude said, was scattered around and irretrievably thrown apart by the centrifugal force of the world's revolutions.

They finished their lunch and kept driving farther, with Abbott at the wheel, the father at his right and Clive in the back. Now they were on their favorite road along the ridge of the mountains. Clive's posture was itself enough to express his disapproval of this nonsense. Abbott seemed to gulp in the road as a drunkard downs whiskey. Suddenly and unexpectedly, Abbott slowed for a turn. "This is a new sign and a new place," he said. He made a sharp turn through a gateway bearing the sign "Quaker Valley Camp Settlement."

Clive came awake with demands. "Now we're off the public highway," he declared. "Can I drive?"

"Wait till we see how this dirt driveway is," his father answered.

It was soon evident the driveway was no training track for a novice. It was, indeed, a severe test of the older brother's skill. Abbott kept on, however, relentlessly: switching, curving, down and up and around. "Slower, slower, slower," his father kept counseling. "Before long we'll have to trade this car for a burro."

"That's what I want," Abbott said grimly. "I'll like it still better when we have to leave the burro behind and go swinging from grapevines!" He hadn't said as much as this since they had left home.

They arrived at the campsite, where the ground was being prepared for cabins. There was no one around. Abbott turned off the ignition and, without a word, started to follow the trail that continued beyond. "Come on, Clive," the father said, "we shan't go far." Clive pouted.

"Wait up," Father Duckwald called to Abbott. The latter stopped momentarily and then went on, more slowly. So they proceeded a mile or two into the backwoods, with Abbott determined, like Columbus, to "sail on, sail on, and on". Clive was the "reluctant dragon". The father was in the middle.

They finally were stopped by a barbed-wire fence. At least, the fence gave the father an excuse for calling a halt. On the return to the car, Clive went ahead, but not so far ahead he didn't have a pretty fair notion of what was going on behind him.

"What's the matter with you guys?!" Abbott demanded of his father with a show of anger. "Where's your spirit of adventure?! I'm going to come back here alone, when I don't have you guys along!"

"Listen," his father said intensely. "There's been enough going-it-alone in our family! More than enough… It's for you to put an end to that. It's for you to make an effort to get along with people – beginning with your family, if you can. That's what growing up is, what it means…"

"You can weep that Mom and I walk in opposite directions… You have cause for weeping… But you have cause for rejoicing as well: We've stuck with you, both of us. Besides, you have an opportunity to do better than your folks…You'll have a wife and children to keep together… Stick together with your brother now. Be his comrade."

They had reached the car, without Abbott endeavoring to argue or protest. They resumed their previous positions. Clive, though, had the look of a cat that has swallowed the canary. In what seemed a jiffy, they covered the distance back to the highway that had taken so long before. Abbott was the first to speak. "Clive, there's a campground just ahead: and I'll pull in there so you can drive." There was no word from Clive, but the father murmured to Abbott, "That's the boy!"

Abbott spied other private roadways close to the public thoroughfare and each time he stopped the car and…

THAT'S GOOD for now. I need another drink and my glands are swollen. So far, Old Man Worth isn't bad. Not bad. Not trite. He is in the tradition of James Thurber. I am in the tradition of Walter Mitty. He writes me. Witty Malter. Witty Malter. Willy Matter? The shooting magpies/Quaker dialectic... Too many ellipses. Too many ellipses...

I weep with laughter at the thought of my father telling me, as a teenaged boy, "You have cause for weeping... But you have cause for rejoicing as well." I cannot explain what my father is, but I have no trouble explaining what he is not. And *that* is not Dad. Not Ellis's nephew, who found my sulking humorous. He used to be an angry man who laughed more than he yelled. Yet he found funny that which often angers others.

I recall now, for you, an incident when I was five. Left to my own devices and my sister's box of school supplies, I glued my father's checkbook to the wall. When he returned home, my dad asked me why I had done it. "I couldn't find the tape," was my response.

He liked that one. I could tell you that I haven't made him laugh since, but I would be lying. I and my very expensive English degree were once (still are?) quite amusing in dad's presence. Nonetheless, he used to love when I got drunk and did my Lady Macbeth impression.

OK. Drink in had, another cigarette lit. Let's go and...

...CHANGED places with Clive. The father remained where he was, giving counsel, "Stay in low: stay in low: not too fast between these trees." It didn't take a lot of this to give Clive a feeling of contentment and competence. After the third or fourth sortie as a driver, he remained in the front seat between his father and brother. The hump on the floor couldn't have allowed his long and growing legs much room, but sitting there was a matter of choice.

The left the smooth highway for a narrow, dirt road which was pretty slippery from the rain, especially on the plentiful, roller-coaster, hills and curves. The driver made no complaint that there was too many in the front seat. The road worked down to the level of a stream liberally sprinkled with beaver-dams[28], and all the adventurers kept a close but vain lookout for the bashful engineers. Trout flashed to the surface of the creek frequently and as frequently evoked exclamations of delight and woefully unreliable estimates of their length and weight. Across the creek were meadows and pastureland and beyond those wooded hills. Ever the same and ever changing, the landscapes exerted a subtle, silent, healing charm.

A porcupine hobbled awkwardly away from the rustic road. "See how he holds his broad, bristled rump high to shield himself," the father cried out.

"Why don't you stop and go back? Clive asked.

"Too late now," Abbott said. He had the car in second gear for safety's sake, but wasn't just creeping along.

Before they knew it, a big, gray, mule-deer was bounding across the road in front of them. Then, leaping as if his legs were pogo-sticks, he cleared a fence between him and a field at the right. Then they saw him join three other, smaller, deer and they all scampered off into the woods.

"Gosh, he was big! Was it a buck or a doe?" Clive asked.

"You answered your own question," said Abbott. "You said 'he'."

"Didn't you see those things sticking up beside his ears?" the father put in. "Those were antlers."

"Oh yes, they grow new ones each year, don't they?"

---

[28] *Liberally Sprinkled with Beaver Dams* will be the title of my next memoir.

"Yes. They grow incredibly fast—an inch a day or something like that," Abbott supplied.

There was a silence as they approached a surfaced highway. Then, when they were back on asphalt, rolling fast toward home, Clive said "Somebody has to reduce the size of the herds, but I don't know whether I'd want to shoot a deer or not... You used to shoot ducks, did you, Dad?"

"Yes, I've hunted and shot most everything, but I never really liked it."

"Oh, Dad... I mean, Abbott, did you know that Quaker Settlement belongs to the Society of Friends? I mean did you know that when you drove there today?" Clive had raised his voice and its shrillness was eloquent of excitement and hot pursuit. The father looked at them both, wonderingly.

"Maybe," Abbott replied. "I don't know... I've heard of the friendly persuasion, of course... That's as old as the hills, but that camp-sign wasn't there last year. You know that." He brought the car to a standstill on the shoulder. "Dad," he said, "will you take over? That winding road wore me out... And, Clive, if you want to sit in front, I'll lie down in the back." They all shifted around.

As they started forward again, Abbott resumed. "Quaker may be just the name of the place for all I know, Clive—like Quaker breakfast foods, Quaker auto oil, and all that."

Clive had lost interest in his question, in Friends, in the antler-crowned king of the forest and all his subjects. Either that or he had plucked the answer from between his brother's words, as a swooping kingfisher snatches his prey from beneath the surface of the water. In any case, he started to sing "Three jolly coachmen, in an English tavern.

Three jolly coachmen—, You sing the upper, Abbott, and I'll sing the lower."

    With their father at the controls and Abbott half-sitting and half-sprawling in the

back seat and Clive turned side-wards, the two sons filled the car, the air, and their

father's ears with music.[29] The car glided swiftly down the gradual Pass with a low swish

below and in front a gentle hum resembling the contented purr of a cat drowsing near a

fireplace on a winter evening.[30]


SCRAWLED weakly at the foot of page eleven: "Typed originally 6/7/61 – Revised

9/22/62."


    I have no further critiques tonight. My glands are swollen and I'm half-jarred.

My toe is aching. Below Beckett. What? Worth.

That last image… that sleepy winter kitty:

Fog rubs back upon window-panes…

Smoke rubs muzzle on window-panes…

Tongue of the evening…

Lingered pools that…

Stand in drains…

Let fall soot fall chimneys…

---

[29] After riding along the road, on both sides of which were the bivouac fires, where they could near the sounds of men talking in French, Dolokhof turned into the yard of the manor house. On reaching the gates, he slid off his horse and went up to a great blazing campfire around which sat a number of men talking loudly. In a kettle at the edge of it something was cooking, and a soldier in a cap and blue cape was on his knees in front of it, his face brightly lighted by the flames, and was stirring it with his ramrod. (Tolstoy, p. 617)

[30] Worth, Ellis, <u>Revolution in the Rain</u> (Unpublished, 1962; printed with permission).

Slipped made a leap…

Soft October night…

June there, then…

December here…

Curled once about the house, and fell asleep.[31]

Yup. That's the one.[32]

---

[31] The above lines, I believe, are truncated bits from the canonical public domain poem "The Love Song of J. Alfred Prufrock" by T.S Eliot. I know that now, but often the work's name escapes me as its lines roll around my mind when sleep arrives.

[32] But a fortnight after his departure, most unexpectedly to the household, she woke up out of this spiritual illness, and began to seem the same as formerly; except that her whole moral nature was changed, just as the faces of children change during protracted illness (Tolstoy, p. 283).

# Chapter 3

*"The sleep of reason brings forth monsters."*

*-Francisco Goya y Lucientes*

## The Deaf Man's Cottage

CERBERUS joined me as my tires popped over snow and gravel toward the house. Other Mom's rural driveway is narrow, winding, and rocky. I drove Char's car[33] slowly so as not to run over the dog, drooling and leaping like a sick gymnast alongside me. I must admit that my eyes were not safely on my path, but fixed on Cerberus.

As my car left the driveway and rolled slowly over Other Mom's front lawn-cum-parking lot, the animal ceased hopping and broke into a calm trot as he gazed, not at me gazing at him, but at my rearview mirror. I could only see his head struggling to float between my open window and the bare trees. He was near drowning but scarcely kept his head within my field of vision as his eyes focused on something behind me. Cerberus ignored me and I couldn't watch anything else.

His head covered just a fraction of my window's space.

Something was missing.

The dog bobbed and spat in the left corner while the rest of my screen showed a reeling white and brown winterscape. There must be someone else. A hunter in search of shot game? A blind man to be led? A frisbee-throwing blonde? Or was Cerberus supposed to be alone in just that corner of my window but the center of my eye?

---

[33] She loaned it to me for a night at the cost of picking up shifts on Christmas Eve and Christmas Day.

As I write this, I prefer the blind man idea. Cerberus is, if nothing else, a humanitarian.

Closing in on the garage, I trilled up Char's emergency brake and stepped out of the car. Cerberus sat at the front driver's side tire panting. I petted hard between his erect ears and walked inside.

"Hoi? Other Mom! I'm here!" I shouted as I entered the mud room through an unlocked door. My voice was stifled by a stack of moldy rainbow life vests.

I wanted to leave already. I hated, and hate, talking to Other Mom in any setting that does not sell alcohol. Part of me also wanted to see that dog again. Cerberus never bothers anyone unless they are coming or going. He doesn't so much protect the Gates of Hell as he yelps hello and goodbye.

"'Ther Mom! You here?"

"Yes, I'm here! I'm getting the rollers out of my hair. Two left. Hold your water. I'll be right out. Grab a beer out the fridge and go outside with the dog. Lay by his dish where you belong." I could faintly hear her giggling into the mirror.

As ordered, I grabbed a beer, a can of something local, cracked it and went outside. The house, its stink, was oppressively sharp. Like Aunt Sis's duller-smelling abode, it is replete with knick-knacks and sundry shit. Other Mom is fond of her late husband's fishing trophies. The walls are covered with taxidermied twenty-five pound Northern Pikes pulled from Canadian lakes during the Eisenhower Administration and three-pound Sunfish posthumously positioned in reenactment of their final moments: Tiny mouths agape to unnatural degrees, trying to suck plastic worms off metal spikes. Unlike the larger Northerns, whose corpses are bent majestically across enormous slabs of driftwood, the Sunfish are condemned, in death, to being permanent symbols of their idiocy.

The house always smells of fish, too. Frankly, I'd rather sit out in the cold.


ON THE back porch, I imagined myself as one of those antebellum, South-of-the-Mason-Dixon-Line moonshiners sitting on an overturned five-gallon bucket. Jeans rolled to mid-shin. No shoes. Wife beater stained, untucked. I imagined this and, despite the sub-zero temperature, I mimicked.

The butt of my shotgun was on the concrete porch. My right hand sweaty around the pump; I applied strong downward pressure, trying to shove my weapon through the dried cement and into the dirt. I imagined myself hunched forward so the barrel – my scepter – hung a foot above the crown of my head. My scapulae protruded into the air like ah! bright wings; I scowled, waiting for that sucker to fly by.

It would be easy to write a story about shooting a rat or a cat or a pig or a boy or a tree trunk or a windshield out. But birds, I tell you. They're unpredictable when they're in the air. Rats and cats and pigs and boys and windshields out are earth-bound. They don't make your eyes bounce.

In Little League, I was a celebrated infielder – third and second, mostly – but I could never play outfield. A fly ball! My eyes shook. The sun gathers to greatness! I duck. The ball thuds hard into the grass behind me. The runner scores from first.

But I'm going to get that sucker today.

I would shoot a rat as he poked his head out from around the corner of Other Mom's house. I don't know if I could shoot a pig, I guess. I could only shoot *at* him. Too human. E-9. In many ways, boys and cats are the same. I have shot windshields out, however. For real.

An exploding windshield gives off quick glares like sheet lightening and also, and this is true of nothing else, possesses zigzag dints and creasings, a sort of fork lightening, too. A shot rat would be so much less dynamic. Just dead and oozing itself out gradually. No flash and dazzle. The dearest freshness deep down things, I guess.

It was cold.

"ALRIGHT, BOY! I'm ready. The rollers are out[34] and the dentures are in. Let's roll." Other Mom looked sharp. Her skinny face projected a thick red lipstick that both accentuated her jagged and brown teeth and shone like the Northern Lights. Her short, tight hair flatteringly matched her teeth in color and, as was inevitably the case when she left the house, irrespective of weather, would soon be covered by blue plastic. Her hands were large and arthritic, just as I imagine Johnny Bench's must be. Her shoes were pink and peep-toed, revealing a dry olive skin and apparently petrified nails brushed brown; her pants were always black and synthetic. I'm sure Other Mom's top was lovely under her windbreaker. Her eyes, artificially large when viewed through her glasses, rattled with astigmatism. "Let's go, boy!"

Other Mom often joked about her dead husband, but I know she cried for him at night. She still made him coffee in the morning. She washed his clothes weekly. "Let's go. Put your shirt and shoes on, Skinny. It's cold." She cannot cook for one.

My car again crunched gravel as we left. Other Mom's head was turned away from me, her eyes brushed over whatever was given them. Mine, again, couldn't get

---

[34] They weren't totally. A pink one hung loosely behind her right ear. But who's it hurting?

away from that hopping, effing dog. Cerberus kept pace until we reached pavement. Then he shrunk in the rearview mirror.

Snowflakes melted off Other Mom's plastic bonnet and the resulting rain dripped at in inconsistent pace onto my emergency brake.

OTHER MOM and I planned to meet Aunt Sis[35] and their mutual friend Sophie at The Deaf Man's Cottage, their local public house. The former proprietor, of whose name I'm unsure, was deaf. Hence…

Of greater consequence to me is that all of the patrons – the sickening majority of whom are old ladies – behave as if they are hearing impaired as well. It is the loudest bar on our adolescent planet. And not a good loud, not *rock concert* loud. It is a chirping, screeching loud. It is *WNBA game* loud.

Upon entering The Deaf Man's Cottage, the young are overwhelmed with a foul potpourri of noises: Glasses clinking against false teeth, cigarette lighters snickering, spilt beer slapping tile, polka. The young must lean across tables and shout at their Other Moms or Aunts Sis. Either that, or avoid verbal communication at all costs – which is generally my chosen route – and nonverbally project an acceptable level of boredom: Just enough to make sure the old ladies keep the free drinks coming.

THE DEAF MAN'S Cottage is not the place for a young man to pick up women. Other Mom thought my compensation for giving her a ride to drink was the opportunity to find a "nice, young girl again." In fact, I think Other Mom was the youngest girl at the Dead Man's Cottage, and doubtless the nicest. Aunt Sis is a mean old cunt who I find lovely.

[35] Sis refused to give me a ride to Other Mom's, so I was forced to beg Char for her car.

Sophie is nice enough, but I've been told she is a repeat felon. Rumor is that Sophie ended her last marriage with a pair of scissors – the very pair that is invariably found in her purse among the mints, keys, and loose string. This assault on Husband Number Three was Felony Number Two. The first was her third DWI.

"Have you a girlfriend yet, Shawn?"

"No, Other Mom."

"Today's your day, Shawn. And mine. It's meat raffle day. Meat spin."

I have no doubt she will cook the pork chop trophy meal for two.


UPON ENTERING the Deaf Man's Cottage, I observed the bartender devouring a burger whose melted cheese topping had nearly split in two and was sagging like a yellow forked tongue to the svelte man's waist, where middling excitement was apparent. Grease and ketchup poured from the cheese like saliva and blood. I stumbled against Other Mom's heel, distracted and, frankly, distressed by the bearded man chewing.

But it was only the special. Fries and pickle chips included, the dry erase board said.

Absolutely horrific.

Drinks were on Other Mom, whose seated friends waved us down, distracting me again from the cannibalism. Aunt Sis and Sophie were sewing and drinking at their table for four.

As Other Mom and I waited for our pints, I turned around to face the public, displaying myself to the ancient. Just in front of me was a youngish woman. She was fairly attractive and apparently here only to, like me, keep older kin company and drunk.

It's so loud in the Deaf Man's Cottage that she and her relative[36] talked in crumpled fingers, stopping every so often to ask if that last gesture meant what they wanted it to. Sign language. They were talking about me. But they knew, somehow, that I didn't know what their hands meant.

Youth – brunette despite her head wrap and a catlike face – liked me. When it was her turn to listen, she dropped her hand under the table (in my plain view), slipped her wedding ring all the way down to the naked fingernail and twirled it like a gilded hula hoop. I know she wanted to fling it to the floor. I know she liked me. I know she was bored and in mourning. Her eyes were dazzling though they never peered my way. She was alive and silent in this din of imminent death.

Other Mom, pints in hand, led me to Aunt Sis and Sophie, who held a magnifying glass and a pair of scissors loosely, like an arrogant outlaw holds his .45s. A clod of grey yarn inadvertently soaked beer. Upon sitting, Other Mom was given this damp mass, the embryonic makings of what is likely today Sophie's granddaughter's doll.

"Here's the doll. You couldn't bring pints, you chiseler?"

"It's lovely. Or it may be one day. And fuck off. You have a fresh beer in front of you, you chiseling little..."

"Stifle it, both of you," Aunt Sis chimed in, ready to spray insults in all directions. "Neither of you are wanting more alcohol. You either, Mister Designated Driver. You smell like my upper lip. And that doll is raggedy. And watch your language. This isn't the library."

"It's not finished yet," Sophie defended. "And Annie likes them limp."

---

[36] An aunt, maybe? The two are clearly comfortable with one another, ruling out the possibility of a mother-daughter relationship.

Instead of lobbing up the obvious retort, I grinned broadly and began staring at the barroom floor just beyond my left thigh. The linoleum was muddied and yellow, mostly covered in peanut shells and grey purses. A lunar setting.

"Did you read Edward's stories?" Sis queried.

"Not yet."

"Here she is, Shawn. Annie's school picture," Sophie injected.
She passed me the small photo between her thumb and index finger. From her middle and ring fingers dangled her open scissors. I took the image, Sophie withdrew and snipped at the doll's foot.

Annie appeared to be a high school junior. The tips of her gelled bangs rose beyond the limits of the photo. She was not embarrassed by her braces, which brightly reflected the light that shone from the ordinarily inconspicuous photographer's luminous umbrella. No acne. No makeup. Nothing.

Sophie is a pointer. She, especially when drunk, has a tendency to put her finger in the faces of her friends when telling them what she thinks about them. When she is with scissors, things can get scary. Occasionally she forgets about the pike in her hand, as if it is an extension of her body, and thrusts the tool dangerously close to the eyes of her pals. This is what I saw when a *dink* lifted my attention from Annie.

Other Mom threw her pint glass in front of her face to shield herself from Sophie's scissors. Sophie, with one thrust, got too close. Her scissors hit the glass, which cracked and spit beer across Other Mom's plastic jacket.

"What the hell, Sophie?! Calm and drop your weapon! I'm just saying, I think a fifteen-year-old doesn't want a fucking homemade doll!

For a few hard moments, Other Mom assessed her droplets. Fighting the desire to brush them away, her arms danced stiffly about like those of a marionettist. "Oh, shoot. I'm all wet! You could have killed me!"

"Oh, shut it. I know what I'm doing. Give me that doll, Sis," Sophie barked as she tucked scissors into her armpit.

Aunt Sis handed what looked like a loose and tiny pile of laundry to Sophie, who snatched it with her safe hand. "You're welcome. Will you cut this, Soph?"

I pulled a pen from someone's purse and wrote on the back of Annie's picture:

*I'm drowning her picture in a glass.*

*Her sketched and outlined eyes*

*Pink and carbonated*

*Just like real life*

*She assured me that*

*Love is not a victory march*

*Her lips to the left of my ear, vibrating*

*I flutter away*

*And drifted not knowing what she meant*

*This morning I find her sleeping downstairs,*

*Naked, hesitant, competing*

*That's how she said goodbye*

*And I won't let her reach the surface for air.*

A pointed pain on the skin of my forehead stopped the new pen. As I peered up, trying to view my brow, Sophie silently and aggressively pointed her closed scissors toward my heart. I gently slipped the pocket-sized photo of Annie between the abutting metal branches. She is Judith and I was nearly Holofernes. Judith, with a grin and a weapon, must avenge her people.


THE DECIBEL level within the Deaf Man's Cottage never falls; nevertheless, the table at which I sat fell silent: Other Mom picked apart her copy of the *Times* with her magnifying glass, Aunt Sis shot dirty looks at her tablemates, and Sophie played with the sinewy doll and clipped anything that came her way. I idled. To my left, two old men ate soup and chuckled malevolently as they crushed handfuls of crackers into their thick, white fare. The younger-looking man – still no doubt an octogenarian – hosted a mouthful of food on his cheek and pointed wistfully at his spoon with crumby fingers. Guarding the utensil, his eyes stared at someone or something across the room. The second man – closer to a corpse – held his sunken and dried face safely inches above his soup and laughed at his partner's spoon.

As I followed Spoon Man's eyes to their focus, mine were led behind the bar, where the burger-eating bartender was being whispered to. He was learning. Some might describe his face as melancholy, but I will not. Instead it appeared pensive, concentrated on something past instead of his informer's words. The whisperer was considerably shorter than his receptacle, who tilted his torso toward the tip-toed latter. The talking man was an animal: Bald with pointing teeth, a greenish hue to the skin, and an open mouth nearly wrapped around the bartender's left ear. With a nod from his witness, the beast backed away and the bartender, carrying a small wicker basket, approached our table.

My three old women, caught up by their existential props, did not notice the man's approach and, in fact, failed to lift their heads until he, shaggy and hovering, greeted them.

"Young ladies."

With this, Other Mom, Aunt Sis, and Sophie each set down their devices and mumbled inaudible responses. One may have asked "How's tricks?" Another may have inquired, "How are you, Billy?" Yet another possible stating, "Hey, you."

I did make out the following:

"How are you young ladies doing today? Anything to eat or just the liquids?"

"Just the jars today. We had lunch earlier as far as you know," Aunt Sis said flirtatiously. "Just the company, the knitting, the culture, the fine lager. This is my nephew Shawn, William."

"Nice to meet you Shawn William," The bearded-man cackled. I grinned tiresomely and shook his offered hand. "Shawn Shook. And to you. How's things?"

"No complaints. William Hidalgo. I just came over to see if you and your lovely ladies would be interested in participating in this afternoon's meat raffle. A dollar a ticket. For the health and the love life? Meat for the spirit and all that…"

"You're Spanish?" I diverted him from meat talk. "How far back?"

"I'm sorry," he craned, his hair at a glacis nearly reaching the pocked floor.

"When did you ancestors arrive from Spain?" I half-shouted.

"No clue. Nobility, though. Ask my mother. Unfortunately... And you? What's Shook?"

"Again?"

"*Shook*! Where does Shook come from?"

"Irish. It's a corruption of the phrase *gach aon mhac máthar acu.*

"Oh, wow. That great. Who wants to win meat?" his attentions were sprinkled around the table, dodging others' like a small dog. "It's for the kids. For the youth hockey. For the future, meat is. We'll spin and you win. Drop the buck. Drop the puck. Eat up. But I don't need to tell you young ladies."

The women each muttered something in the affirmative and started digging for cash. Other Mom and Aunt Sis each passed their fivers to Billy. Or Willy.

As Sophie reached into her purse for what I would shortly discover to be two dollars, I surreptitiously grabbed her photo of Annie off the table, momentarily held it between my knees, took one last glance and dropped her into my half-full pint glass. At first, she just floated on top. But after my sip, Annie dropped. She became blurry, as if holding her hands over my face. Maybe she was beautiful.

"Well, there we have it," Bill stated stoutly after handing out the tickets and pocketing the cash. "Good luck to you ladies. Straight from the butchers, yeah?" As he turned away, Billy's long, gray hair swung up toward the ceiling in thick strands; he was what the Spanish would call a *cabrón*. He walked bowlegged and seemingly floated like fog above the purses that dotted the floor of the Deaf Man's Cottage. That is, until he reached the next table and began, again, proselytizing.

"Real nobility?" I shouted at Billy, but it was lost in the murmur

"Will you cut this string, Soph?" And she always did.

I saw Annie's profile in my drink and grew disgusted. The chemicals. The ink. The bacteria. I needed a new drink. With legs spread and arms spread far apart, I abandoned my neck muscles and dropped my head back over the wooden chair back, feigning boredom.

"Would you like a pint, Shawn? I'm about to make a run. One more, huh?" Other Mom asked on cue.

"Yeah, yeah. That's fine. I'm fine. I'll have one."

"Good stuff. Just let me finish reading this article. The crops and all." Other Mom drew the magnifying glass back to her face.

A group of old men had gathered near a long luncheon table at barroom's end. Carrying sacks of meat, it clumped itself into a ball forcing defrosting prizes onto the already crowded stall. One man, with eyes obviously rolled back into his skull, was in pain as another in a gaudy-brimmed hat forced a roast into his back, the former's pelvis crushed by the poker table's edge. The victim's mouth shot open like that of a Sunfish as the table began compressing his surely artificial hips. The other men peered stupidly back into the crowd to make sure no one was paying attention, like adults ensuring children don't discover Uncle Phil is Santa Claus tonight. Make sure they can't see him. They can't know this year.[37]

These Meat Men, stuck in the dark back corner of the Deaf Man's Cottage were apparently unnoticeable to the rest of the patrons, who saw, if anything at all, only blurs

---

[37] In executing this Santa ruse, it is essential to select the adult male who both has no children of his own and is disliked, or at least found to be of mild interest, by the young. As a result, when the moment of excitement - Santa's entrance – arrives, no children begin looking for this adult to share with him the news that "Santa's here!" In the case of the Shook family, no one of any age would ever think of sharing interesting information with Phil.

of blacks, grays, browns, ochres. The plastic bags that carried the meats created an occasional white splash. Behind the ball of men was a queue of other meat carriers, many of whom wore black stocking caps or hoods. Only one was female. She wore a long black dress, a grey veil, and hid her meat bag under a shawl.

The wet plastic bags kept piling up. And, I hadn't thought it possible, but the room's shrill tumult rose slowly as the mound swelled.

As the Deaf Man's Cottage began to fill in anticipation of the raffle, the bartender, Billy, got busy. The line at the bar was three, at some places four, deep. Sophie noticed this and motioned for the two others to follow her. The three women walked across the bridge of purses, purchased their liquids after a three minutes' wait, sipped, and were healed. And *yo lo vi.*

Light was being poured through windows at the rear of the barroom. That throng of dark men had just completed piling their sacks of steaks, chops, and other cuts onto the table. This meat mountain nearly reached the ceiling. It stood no less than nine feet high, though, admittedly, its base table stood at least three feet from the floor. The raffle trophies had begun a rapid defrost and would soon, I was certain, begin to stink. This new stench would mingle with, but would be unlikely to conquer, that of the cottage's rapidly expanding and steadily aging patrons. The result would be unbearable: Rotting flesh, lager, Old Spice, Polygrip, and Pall Malls. The reek had not yet been achieved, but firmly held second place on the list of anticipated sensory experiences, far behind that which had long ago secured the top spot: Gripping food in victorious and wrinkled hands after the raffle ticket hit.

Shafts of sunlight were converting our blacks, browns, grays, and ochres to yellow ochres, oranges, pale blues, and light browns. The clientele chatted, stood, and swayed like grass blades in wind. Women dragged purses across the damp floor like sticks across beach sand, inadvertently writing their stories. I could see their letters, but could not read; I could not follow.

The sight of that fully illuminated Martello Tower of *feoil* clearly frightened Sophie, who, draped in red and with blurry face – not unlike her Annie, whose colors were running – clutched my shoulder with her left hand and forced me to point at the meat prizes, as if surprised. The decibel level in the room was now maddening. I, drifting in many ways, directed Sophie's attention to the mass of animal because she, holding me and beer, could not do it herself. Her head turned away. The men who had constructed the meat heap now had their seats. Their heads were covered; they were drinking and rubbing their tickets.

It was only after seven winning numbers[38] had been called that ankles were beginning to be submerged in the thaw. Hoar-frost had melted and water was accumulating. The puddling was only occurring around the meat table and had not yet reached us. But it was only a matter of time. One of the men sitting near the mound had, ignorant of the dripping bags, accused another nearby of urinating at an inappropriate time and location. The accused took exception to this indictment and challenged the complainant to a duel. Both men grabbed wooden spoons off their table and, shin-deep in unfrozen chest freezer ice and animal juices, violently slapped each other with their

---

[38] 5, 27, 78, 3, 30, 17, and 46. Aunt Sis walked away with a plastic bagful of mutton. And, as she quipped, she got it "for nuttin'". This, of course, was not the case. She paid five dollars for as many meat raffle tickets.

utensils as the raffler continued calling out, barely audible: *83, 12, 33, 46, 78, 10, 6, 55, 49...*

By now the crowded barroom was full of men and women with fresh dinner. The table to my left held at least five men hovering over their booty reading the brown paper bag that held it: The sack was littered with at least a dozen phrases, each of a different tongue, that translate to the English "Welcome!" The winner, central at the table, wore a white shirt and was well lit, literally and figuratively. The four (five?) others wore black and stayed out of the ceiling fan light. To my right, a man had taken a steak out of its bag and had begun fondling it. His two female companions were in tears, laughing with neon teeth.

Sis had tucked mutton into her purse. I had tucked damp Annie into my pocket.

It had become difficult to breathe in The Deaf Man's Cottage, what with the cigarette smoke, rancid meat, and rising water level. The melt had submerged every table in the place and was now just below my nipples. Other Mom knocked back the last of her pint and announced it was late, and time to go. The three old women and I waded in procession through the bar to the exit, followed by hundreds of others dressed in black.[39]

Outside the world was cold and dry. Aunt Sis and Sophie walked to their cars without saying goodbye. Other Mom and I fell into Char's car, frozen solid. Its heater coughed and the radio told us that the murder of a Hmong hunter had eastern Wisconsin on edge, the United States had launched air strikes on Somalia, the price of oil had fallen

---

[39] Mariu Mariam once wrote that the Spanish Inquisition was "not only the guardian of society's moral welfare but was also a sort of thought-police... A melancholy, dark landscape is the setting for this procession of severe ecclesiastical figures...the figures are deformed and seem more animal than human." (The Black Paintings (Aldesea, 2004) p. 30)

to $56 dollars per barrel, and a Houston boy had hanged himself while mimicking Saddam Hussein's execution.

Other Mom sniffled at this news and peered out the dark window, silent all the way home as Char's tires crunched the snow. With high beams on, Cerberus met us at the foot of the driveway and floated beside the car, again, until we reached the driveway. Silent and defrosted, we walked through the mud room, beneath the mounted fish, and passed out.

# Chapter 4

*"Only crazy for what I haven't got... like any drowning, starving man."*

*-Henry Green*

## Self Talk

SUNLIGHT shone off the railroad tracks as I drove home. The glare was racing, beating me. But the farther the car threw me the more the brilliance fell behind. I drove southeast, forgetting momentarily. By the time I recalled, it was gone.

The untangled tracks, so long running parallel to the highway, had tailed off.

Hung over, stinking of smoke and animal parts, I drove toward the Twin Cities; a book on tape played[40] but I wasn't listening. As I glided over black ice, I wrote the following on the inside of my skull with a magic marker:

I AM 32 years old.

I have had five homes since birth, all within earshot of tracks. It is well known that trains are loud.

Tracks are, too, when run upon.

My first home, that in which I was raised, was and is located two suburban blocks from a freight line whose trains carried mostly honey.

---

[40] *The Odyssey*? For whatever reason, I associate the following tale with a "rosy-fingered dawn".

The trains are a rolling horizon for stopped traffic: Douglas Drive midafternoon traffic. Cars and trucks immobile and quiet for tens of minutes as the honey passed. When standing close to these tracks as the tankers filled with sweet fluids approached, the sound emitted was a low, grinding rumble. Audible hunger. Then a steady swallow. Then an imperfect roll call. Then that stereotypical chug. Then God's icy wind.

In the winter, this procession of sound is pitched up just slightly. Everything is pitched up in the Minnesota cold. The train glides by, inches from my face, closer yet to my bare toes, creating a manmade chill.

The honey logo – a fat, grinning bee skipping rope – is too near my eyes.


STRADDLING THEIR perpendicular wooden supports, I know this:

If the tracks grumble and crunch, the trains carry, slowly, grain.

Is the train convulsing? Screeching not from pain but from burden?

Yes. This time it's an Amtrak: People who pay to move slowly, but faster than their honeys and wheat.

Time and air pass; all else is still. I crack open one eye, prompted by the conductor's frantic whistles. The passengers stare at me confusedly, some angrily. In truth, I never can decipher what they think of me buzzing by.

I close the eye again until they pass.

And now I can see that river again.


In my twenties I moved to London.

My garret was in Camden Town, near its National Rail station. Trains and tracks in London are not like those in Minnesota: One must pay, or risk apprehension, to stand near the London rails. But, after imbursement, one is *encouraged* to stand near the pits.

The sounds emitted from Britain's tracks are the same whether one is atop the yellow line or in bed. My first night in Camden, near sleep, I imagined leaning into the passing train and absorbing a fresh charge.

Sound travels well in London. It maintains fidelity despite distance and urban hurdles. All sounds soldered to one another, keeping their original distinctive clamor. London air circulates and throbs, being sucked into and out of lungs, carrying the smoke from rollies and Mayfairs, from buses and Peugots and canon. In and out of the cafés and windows, through the end doors of the train cars and under my feet. Through my fingers, down my throat, and around the millions of necks.[41]

The National Rail tracks crack like snow under a plastic sled. From inside, the sounds are not dissimilar to those trains in the cartoons I watched as a boy in Minnesota. Two blocks from the real trains carrying the real honey to you. Close your eyes.


I MET A GIRL at a pub. Her eyes were veiled by her own black hair as she attempted to steal my tray. I ashed on the cuticle of her right thumb. She stuck her tongue out at me. She showed me her eyes and my brow hopped. We decided to smoke together.

Two months later we moved into a tiny flat in Kilburn. It was yards from the Underground tracks, which, as they are in most London suburbs, above ground.

---

[41] The steam hissed. Someone cleared his throat.
No one left and no one came
On the bare platform. What I saw
Was Adelstrop—only the name.

During our first night at our new room, I sat at my rented desk with the window open as my girlfriend slept (she always falls asleep first). I heard war. A battle. Starships. Heroes. Heroines. Death. Exemption. Panzers. Plotting. Slipping. Commanding. And the battle repeated itself (each was so brief!) every three minutes.

The next morning, taking the Jubilee line into work, I eagerly awaited new conflicts.

NEXT TRAIN: STRATFORD     1 MINUTE

And here it is. *Zap! Zap! Pyoo! Ping! Peez!*

Eyes closed. I can feel the train bend into the tracks, whipping them violently from side to side.

Imagine fanning a loved one rapidly with an enormous, flimsy hunk of sheet metal. That's the sound.

I get on.

Lead poisoning.

I would never die that way. But I understand.

My wife (the Kilburn girl) still falls asleep first and I still listen to the tracks across the baseball diamond from our new home in Minnesota. But I've never stood next to these tracks. I've never dared approach them. I promised her I wouldn't. That was right after I proposed and just before she said yes.

We've been in our apartment a year now and I've kept my word. I did wander into center field once, drunk, I think. Now I just listen and imagine from inside my home; I *guess* what this train carries. That one. The next. This one.

When the train passed our house last night, I heard the tracks quake as my wife laughed staccato in her sleep.

Some dream. I deserve to be this alone.

## Self Portrait

AT HOME, headache and eyes clear, I stare into the mirror. Inches below my armpits, my ribs show through my skin, incongruously, mere inches from a substantial belly. When I was nineteen, I had tattooed on my stomach the thirty-fourth hexagram of *The Book of I Ching*. Then, I was svelte and six-packed. Now, the rotundity of my stomach forces the inked character to protrude at its middle and bend around its edges, making it look exactly like the AT&T logo.

My eyes have grown greener, less blue, since my youth. My hair is darker, maybe mousy. My arms are thin and covered with about a dozen coaster-sized tattoos including the head of Felix the Cat and a pedestrian swirly design that I now, deeply embarrassed by this empty signifier, tell curious observers that it is a modern variation on the engravings that dot Newgrange.

My right nipple – both on my body and in the mirror – is calloused and larger than the left one due to an old infection from a shoddy piercing. I broke my clavicle once skateboarding. Just above the mole on my left cheek is a scab from an old shaving error.

I didn't work today. But I do tomorrow, so I had better get started.

Like any child, it takes more than just coaxing to bring my sleep into sight. One must buy her nice presents. So I drink. And after three shots of Jameson, I find a Sharpie and write the following on my bathroom wall:

# Feats of Strength

SO MY GIRLFRIEND sent me a letter today. It said I miss you. She didn't sign her name, but the handwriting was unmistakable: Loopy letters, with an obese heart after the sentence instead of a period. Someone covered the envelope's return address with Wite-Out. I wonder if she did it, or if it was someone else. Jenny hasn't seen me in nineteen months. But I've seen her here and there.

We used to play pool at O'Neill's and have beers. She was terrible at pool and she made me feel terrible, too. Jenny could never find the pockets, but always provided me with a shitty leave.

"Bitch," I would call her – just kidding though – after seeing the crappy leave.

"Bugger you, then," she'd say back. I never knew if she really meant it.

One of those nights at O'Neill's Jenny went home without me and she never saw me again. It's been nineteen months, but she's still my girlfriend because we never broke up; and like this note says, she still misses me. When she comes back, I'll call her a bitch and smile: Just messing around, of course.

Getting that letter from Jenny got me wanting to play pool. It also got me wanting to call Gary, partly because he was a poor pool player and partly because he always laughed at me for calling Jenny my girlfriend instead of my ex.

I couldn't remember Gary's number, but eventually found it buried my cell phonebook. I had filed it under his last name (PROCTOR) and not his first name (GARY). I didn't even know I knew his last name.

Gary wasn't married and was usually available to play pool and drink. I was sure that would be the case tonight, and it was. I hopped on the bus and headed to The Bakery, which was another local pool hall, actually.

I WAS GLAD I decided to take the bus to the Bakery (and not my truck) because, while I was reading Jenny's letter, it had begun to snow. This was the first snow of the year. There's nothing worse than driving home after a few beers in the first snowfall. No matter how long you've lived around this stuff, you forget how to drive in it every year.

As I shuffled down the aisle and the bus pulled away from my stop, the roof brushed under tree branches that were hanging over the road. I heard the wood scraping metal from inside the warm bus and saw the snow that had collected on the branches fall to the ground. If you grew up around snow, you can – just by looking at it – tell the difference between the snow that falls from the sky and the snow that falls from something else.

I got in a little trouble on the bus. I was staring at an old woman who was wearing an eye patch. I was trying to figure out what happened. Where it had happened? Had it hurt? Who has her eye? The usual. She caught me staring at her and loudly, from across the length of the bus, told me to fuck off, which I can understand. So I quickly turned my head the other way, then back in her direction (without eye contact) as if trying to stretch my neck or crack it. Then I started massaging my own shoulders, but they weren't sore. I just didn't want to appear nosy.

My stop was up so I walked past the one-eyed woman and tried to crack my neck one last time before hitting the door. When I was outside, I stepped into a snowfall that was heavier than it was when I got on the bus, but still light enough to melt when it hit my hair.

I looked like a greaser when I saw Gary at the bar; my hair was slicked back and I just happened to be wearing a leather jacket. Gary had made sure a beer was waiting for me, so to thank him (and to show off my new hair) I struck a Fonzie pose:

1) FINGERS INTO GUNS POINTING AT HIM

2) LEGS SPREAD AND STAGGERED

3) CROOKED SMIRK

4) PULL THE TRIGGERS

5) POP THE COLLAR

6) "AAAEEYYYY!"

Gary turned away from me laughing, so I shook my wet hair at him like a dog, but it wasn't that wet, so it didn't get his attention. I decided to sit down at the bar, sip my new beer, stare at the mirror behind the bottles of booze and not blink until I decided to light my first cigarette.

There weren't any open pool tables, so Gary and I decided to talk.

"Jenny sent me a letter," I said.

"Oh yeah? What'd she have to say? Where the hell is she anyway?"

"She says she misses me, and is trying to get up enough money to take a bus back home, she says. She says she's sorry. She also told me to say hi to Gary!"

I waved my hand crazy with my eyes crossed and smoke pouring out of my nose.

"Sheeeeeeit. She didn't say nothing to Gary," Gary said.

"Any women in your life yet?" I asked.

Gary told me that he had a new Harley Davidson shirt (sleeveless), an American flag bandana and a pair of those Magnum P.I. sunglasses, and that his name was Jack. Some nights he would put on this outfit and tell people his name was Jack and he was from New York originally. Just here on business, he'd say. When people asked what his business was, he told them he owned a drywall company. Z's Drywall, he said.

"Someone asked me once why I called it Z's because that would mean that I would always be at the end of the phone book. I told them that if you read it backwards, I was at the front. Then I told them that, hell, I wasn't even in the book."

I told Gary he was crazy.

"Works, too!" he said.

Gary said he got a bunch of women coming up and talking to him when he was Jack. He told me they'd walk up to his bar stool, trying to start conversation, but he wouldn't say a word to them. Wouldn't even look at them. Then they'd go away ignored, offended and overweight, he said.

Looking over my beer I saw a pool table had opened, so I grunted with a mouthful of beer, picked up my cigarettes, got up, swallowed and told Gary come on.

I racked without asking or being asked because then Gary would be forced to break. I wanted Gary to break because there's no way he'd knock any balls in off the break. That way I'd have first shot at solids. The only way I could ever win was if I was solids.

That's exactly how it worked out. Gary broke, barely; no balls went in and I had the bright purple ball lined up perfectly with the corner pocket. Loser buys the next round. I knocked it in (with authority, I might add), then sank the yellow one before

muffing on the on the green ball. I hit Gary's stripe first anyway. No slop.

I stepped back and lit a cigarette.

"No pressure," I told Gary. I always liked to get in his head when we played pool.

But my comments usually didn't bother him. As he leaned over the table, his long black

hair blocked the eight ball from my view. He sank a stripe, but scratched.

I had to set my cigarette on the edge of the table while I lined up my next shot.

Orange ball, corner pocket. I sank that shot and the green one before I picked my

cigarette back up and took a drag. Gary stood near the other corner pocket, resting his

crotch on the edge and shaking his head.

I dropped the red and blue balls before accidentally hitting in Gary's fourteen.

"Your shot."

As I finished off my cigarette and beer, I saw a woman off in the corner I thought

awfully beautiful. She was out of place. Long, black hair. Tall with open-toed shoes that

threw leather straps around her ankles. She looked powerful and out of place. Her teeth

were as white as the snow outside before it melted on me. I knew she had a good job by

the way her black coat hung. She was talking on a cell phone and staring right at me. But

I wasn't sure if she meant to look at me like that or if she was just zoning out. Most

people stare at nothing when they're talking to someone. Our eyes locked for a long time,

and then hers shot up and away and she started laughing. She was loud as hell. The way

her eyes rose, I read them like one of those games of strength at the carnival where you

slug something and the metal pellet shoots up and hits a bell. That's what her eyes looked like, that metal pellet flying away. I must be strong. If I slugged her foot with a hammer, I'd have teddy bears.

"Your shot," yelled Gary. He was getting impatient.

Gary must've knocked a couple balls in during that turn. I was still beating him, but only by two balls. As a matter of fact, Gary must've knocked in my seven.

"Did you knock in my seven?" I asked.

"Yeah. I was on a roll, too."

All I had left was a fairly easy shot at the eight ball in the side pocket. The opening still worried me though. I wasn't very good with side pockets.

But I sank it. The cue ball jumped up and away from the pocket and rolled to a stop in the middle of the table, barely nudging one of Gary's stripes for good measure. I won, but I would buy the drinks. After all, I told Gary, you had one waiting for me when I walked in.

We sat down at an open booth, had a beer, probably four cigarettes each and talked more about Jenny, Jack, work, same old. Gary offered to give me a ride home, saying he didn't trust the people on the bus this time of night.

When we walked out of the Bakery, the snow was coming in from every direction, and thick. I, drunk, looked up into the sky at the swirling flakes big as cats. This is serious, I thought. Beautiful and serious. We could barely see Gary's truck from where we were, partly because it was tough to see with all the snow and partly because the blue of Gary's truck was almost gone.

He and I ran to the truck stiff-legged, with our hands in our pockets. We were getting them warm because we knew in a few seconds were going to be brushing the snow off Gary's truck with them. We didn't have any gloves. We just shoved enough away so Gary could see out the important windows: Windshield, driver's side, back.

We hopped in and started rubbing our hands together with our shoulders raised up by our ears. Gary turned over the ignition and flicked up the heat. The engine sounded good but the heater wheezed. Gary pumped the gas pedal, still in park. We didn't drink nearly enough to keep us warm on our own.

The snow started coming down harder when we got on the road. I couldn't see anything beyond the windshield but white. No trees, no branches, no people, no buildings, no buses, not even the other cars. The weatherman said whiteout conditions were to be expected throughout the evening across the metropolitan area and that driving was not advised unless completely necessary. Gary was scared to death behind the wheel, leaning so far forward that the tip of his nose was closer to the windshield than his knuckles. He never blinked.

My cell phone rang. It wasn't Jenny. It was my mom wondering if I was OK in the blizzard. I told her Gary was driving me home and that I'd call her when I walked in the door. She asked if the roads were bad. I said I didn't know because I wasn't driving and I couldn't see any roads from where I sat. She told me she loved me and instructed me to be careful. I gave her my love, replied that by doing nothing I *was* being careful, and assured her that I would not allow this little obstruction to prevent me from seeing her.

I TOOK another shot of Jameson - my seventh - lit a cigarette, massaged my inflated

glands and finished the story with these words, applied to the left jamb of my bathroom

doorway:


I have dreamt
of you,
baby.
Not your face,
just a phone call.
But today
you burn me.
Like
ant
under
micro-
scope
I
smoke.

# Chapter 5

*"In order to protect himself from any possible danger that might result from their interpretation, [Goya] only kept a series of proofs, to which he gave these vague titles."*

*-Xavier de Salas*

## The Path

WORLD wanderers and wayfarers are irresistibly drawn, they say, back to their birthplace and the haunts of their childhood.[42] Criminals respond to some strange, strangling, compulsion which pushes and pulls them to the scene of their most outrageous, revolting, dastardly deed[43], be it their earliest, most distant villainy. Something similar doubtless accounts for my strolling against my better judgment along that "river walk" at Sonora Springs.

I have nothing against "river walks" as such. I have enjoyed ambles past the bookstalls that line the beloved Seine of Paris. Scores of thousands of soldiers and sweethearts have held hands along the charming capricious, strip of concrete in that quaint San Antonio of our own Texas. Multitudes of nature-lovers have exclaimed in ecstasy at the wondrous warblers glimpsed on trips on the restored or preserved towpath bordering the old canal, which, in turn, parallels the Potomac and I thoroughly approve the humane political sentiments which moved the second Roosevelt to sire such projects. But there's a difference in walks![44]

---

[42] History, Stephen said, is a nightmare from which I am trying to awake. (Joyce, James, Ulysses (Penguin, 1992) p. 42)
[43] This alliteration is affecting me.
[44] Blazes Boylan's smart tan shoes creaked on the barfloor where he strode.(Joyce, p. 340)

At the time I ventured upon it, I remembered when that rustic road at Sonora Springs had been built on the margin of Monument River; which, in most seasons of the year, isn't a river at all, but a sandy, half-dry creek. The job was a darling of the WPA, but nobody else loved it, at least no one among the citizenry. Even the workmen who piled and fastened flat stones against the twenty-foot high banks of the stream and strewed pebbles to make a footpath and bicycle trail beside the steep walls and every Saturday collected perforated checks the color of robins' eggs – they didn't like it. So, after all the ceremonies of completion, the ribbon-cutting, the flash-bulb photographs, the speechifying and all that, the parkway fell into almost perfect disuse.

Though I had been gone for years from Sonora Springs – to wars and to such quixotic adventures as peace offers and glorifies under dozens of different, ridiculous, respectable, names – I remembered the origins of the path. I recalled, also, the stony, silent, loneliness of its setting – far from down-town with its theaters, cars, lights, cafes, pedestrians... I should have shunned it like the plague... I was no dumber than those who used their heads and stayed away. I did, indeed, have the presence of mind to debate whether at so late an hour I would have time enough to be safely back on a well-lighted street before the evening sun and its radiant after-effects were lost beyond the hump of the dark-ridged mountains across the tirelessly hurrying serpent of water. I argued the matter with myself and lost the decision.

I crossed San Miguel Street where the tennis courts are, and turned my back on the only portion of the path enjoying any semblance of popularity among the townspeople... I don't mean that by heading north I was throwing in my lot with the vagrants, loiterers, and idle riff-raff such as is common in the blighted areas of the larger cities... No, the direction I took was simply lonelier, more starkly naked to the ominous visage of the breathless, waiting, darkly-looming mountains. In each direction there was foliage at the edge of the path away from the bank of the stream, but the course I took had more scattered, old trees which had been trimmed to the point of amputation following a recent, disastrous, unseasonable snowstorm. These high stumps were anything but symbols of phallic glory – mute, anguished, agonized, testimony, rather, of decapitation or other frightful visitation.

This was July. I had had a late afternoon dinner, but the time now was six o'clock surely, maybe later. The sun was low, but it was impossible to say whether its rays were being cut off by mountains or merely blocked by the dark clouds which then capped the jagged ramparts to the west.

I wasn't walking briskly. I wouldn't say slowly, either. Receptively is perhaps the word for it. I soaked in the atmosphere: and took note that a sudden sally from the bushes and over the bank I'd go. The spring run-off from the melting snows of the high slopes was over and the water wasn't deep enough to be a real danger: more often than not the stream didn't touch its banks on this side. It was, however, swift—and all streams not yet free from the spell of their mountain origin are an unknown quantity. All we natives – hill-billies, if you will – know that.

I spied a man coming my way. He was wearing a long-sleeved white shirt and I felt that his genteel attire was some guarantee of good conduct. I chanced to be wearing a short-sleeved blue-and-brown plaid sport-shirt myself, but from a distance I guessed we both belonged to the same fraternity and were, in some vague manner, bound together by a tight "old school tie". I put on a smile with which to greet the passerby. His dark eyes were sternly, if not madly, fixed and set under a beetling brow and he looked neither to the right nor to the left; certainly not at me. He plodded past at a furious pace, in no mood for amenities of any sort, however brief and fleeting.

Two boys came from behind me on bicycles. There was room for them to travel abreast but not to do so and still pass me. I had the first intimation of their presence when one of the riders turned his front wheel in the pulverized rock so as to get in line with his buddy. The scraping sound startled me just a bit, but of course, I immediately grasped there was no cause for alarm from behind. There was no boisterous give-and-take on the part of the cyclists. They weren't in frenzied haste, but nevertheless gave the impression that laughter and high spirits were absolutely foreign to their daily rounds and accustomed course of conduct.

A massive stone affair with steps going up to a roofless overlook displaced the usual shrubbery at my right. On a rude and ponderous arch was, as I knew, a bronze inscription giving the date the park path, complete with its overlooks, benches and crude tables, had been opened to the public – and giving, as well, the names of the numerous officials entitled to credit for the benefaction. Beneath the plaque, built into the rough, rugged, grotesque, observation post, was a "love-seat" wide enough for four to six persons. A young couple, thoroughly absorbed in themselves – in furious embrace, but still upright on the stone seat—were somewhat taken aback at the sound of my approaching footsteps... It was light enough for me to notice that.

I went on past for, say, the length of a long city block, to a point where the shrubbery gives way and the path opens up on the right into an unused picnic plot. Then I turned around... I was half-way back to the overlook when I again saw the amorous pair.

This time the man, who was taller and thinner than I had realized, had lifted the well-built, bosomy, young woman in his arms as if the two were newly married and he was going to carry over the threshold... She was kicking, but not vehemently, not angrily – more as if, her knees prettily together, she were taking a convenient opportunity for showing her upthrust legs – that is, her shins, calves and feet.[45] Her kicks up and down from the knee were lusty, through, at that – rather rhythmic. She had good legs.

The impulsive lovers quickly disappeared into the woodiness which began where the structure left off... I speculated a bit, in my ignorance, on what to make of the girl's wearing toreador pants under the circumstances, but my speculations came to nothing. I pricked up my ears as I came up to and passed the place of the couple's disappearance from sight, but I could hear not sighs, and, of course, no screams.[46] I'm not as ignorant about everything as about toreador pants.

If it was dark enough for seduction, it was too dark for a stroll, but the nearest exit was the one by the tennis courts at San Miguel Street, so I kept going. It was rather twilight than dark. At one of the wide, shallow, spaces in the river, a big, fierce-looking dog was chasing birds – for the most part, shrieking kildeer – which flew low over the water. He would wheel abruptly and snap his jaws in anticipation as his intended victims turned and careened away. He appeared to have no master. Surely the dog had the intelligence to appreciate the practical futility of his antics, but there was no air of sportive play about his pursuit. He gave up the chase of one bird or set of birds to leap

---

[45] *O, Mary lost the pin of her drawers.*
*She didn't know what to do*
*To keep it up*
*To keep it up*
(Joyce, p. 96)
[46] Here, on the manuscript and in a surprised hand, Ellis wrote, "I didn't expect screaming."

after others with the savage earnestness of a being possessed. He had the lean, hungry, demonic look of a wolf and his front shoulders actually partook of the beige coloring of his wild cousin. But he was a dog; no mistaking that. Too active to be rabid, I judged. In any event, the beast confined his attention to the prey skimming near the water's surface and ignored all else.

The light, slight, breeze which had kept me company up to then had died away. I can't say just when; but gone, now, were the mixed, meagre, tantalizing fragrances of earth, mold, unseen flowers, hazel bushes, cleansing pine and intoxicating juniper. Gone was the soughing, soothing, saddening rustle of needles and fronds. In this solemn stillness might be anything: warning, invitation, grim reminder. The very sky might sooner yield its ultimate secrets than this narrow fortress of the unknowable. Here was a hush beyond the infinite, insolent, invasions before which the serenity of parlors and the intimacies of bedrooms meekly surrender. This was Day welcoming Night with its reign of visions and its intimations of reality.

Then, at a stone's throw, I saw a man coming toward me and I watched him, favorably impressed: very, very favorably impressed – with his medium-build, his gait, his bearing, such things. Right while I was looking, before my Goddam nose, it happened; so quick it was like a dream; so sudden and senseless it's beyond belief; so noiselessly it was deafening. They pushed him over the bank and were gone. A man and a woman, came out of the bushes: not the same ones, I think, I hope. The woman was thinner and wearing a light skirt – t he way I saw it.

I fished the man out and all alone I carried him back up a bank I couldn't have climbed without him.[47] He was dead... Right there with nobody but me, he was dead... His clothing was damp, but he couldn't have drowned there where he fell. I lit a match to see his face. A handsome man; a handsome man; and yet I swear by all the Gods above he looked like me and about my age and I have no brother; and if I live till I die I'll never forget it; and I laid him on a park bench, squashed his hat under his head for a pillow, and left him... What with one thing and another, I didn't dare call for the police – nor tarry.

Now you tell me why I ever went near that Goddam path... No good could come of it, and I knew it, knew it, knew it, till the end of time and the resurrection of the dead, and all that we can ever expect here-below. And so that's the way it is, the long and the short of it, and more long than short, if you ask me; the path to perdition; and all the crooked, rutted routes of the wobbly, wobbling, wobbling world... What other path is there?! Now you tell me... Tell me, tell me, tell me!![48]

7/8/61

# Running

I MUST admit that my eyes, while reading the last paragraph, had been bouncing between the paper and my fish tank. The afternoon sun had ripped through my closed

---

[47] Mourners came out through the gates: woman and a girl. Leanjawed harpy, hard woman at a bargain, her bonnet awry. Girl's face stained with dirt and tears, holding the woman's arm looking up at her for a sign to cry. Fish's face, bloodless and livid.

   The mutes shouldered the coffin and bore it in through the gates. So much dead weight. Felt heavier myself stepping out of that bath. (Joyce, p. 127)

[48] Worth, Ellis, The Path (Unpublished, 1961; printed with permission).

curtains and shot through the tank, whose water was a light catcher, emitting a new and rippling radiance[49] across the couch and transcripts. Even Sam is squinting.

Tossing papers aside, I drape fish food over the surface of the water. Lunch for the tetra runs from its point of contact outward, to the edges of tank, scattering across the surface like something that doesn't start with *s* – how about... video footage of an exploding... whatever. My starter fish[50] confines its attention to the flakes of prey skimming the water's surface and ignores all else.

Speaking of confinement, the tank is covered in a story, which you may read later, that both occupies my living fish and obscures its eleven dead compatriots.

The walls, too, in my apartment are beginning to fill with words. I would like to believe they are well chosen, but, admittedly, my willingness to edit those over which I have doubts is absent: Altering a word written in permanent marker on a rented wall is more painstaking than doing the same with paper and a Cold War-era typewriter. My spelling and grammar are impeccable; my frequent use of the semicolon gives readers, or would give readers, the impression of unsullied punctuation skills.

One day, someone will read me. But today, I have to work. I'm already late, but I refuse to leave this room until I witness this fish-fuck eating. It hasn't touched a thing. Just staring as manna drifts down.[51]

The tank belongs to my cousin Tony, Aunt Sis's youngest. The fish were my idea. Last month, I think, Tony asked me via his mother if I would look after his fish while he

---

[49] Darn you, Uncle!

[50] We purchase starter fish with the intent of killing them. They are, simply, nickel fish that are the first to inhabit new tanks. Their post in life is to soak up fatal levels of ammonia in the new water and create a benevolent bacteria. Following the deaths of starter fish, the tank is safe for new, prettier, more expensive species.

[51] A cloud began to cover the sun slowly, shadowing the bay in deeper green. It lay behind him, a bowl of bitter waters. (Joyce, p. 9)

went away on business.[52] Then I asked him with my eyes to ask again yes and then he asked me would I yes to say yes my mountain flower and first I put my arms around him yes and drew him down to me so he could feel my breasts all perfume yes and his heart was going like mad and yes I said yes I will Yes.

He dropped off the vat last week. It was empty.

I took it upon myself to fill it and... Oh! There it goes. My tetra, bolting in a zigzag toward the surface, with eyes bulged and mouth pursed, sucked a soggy flake into itself.

I have to get to work.

The lone surviving tetra – Ellis, we'll call him – usually, habitually, flutters near the surface in search of something. S/He flits about, almost exclusively, in the near left corner (from my perspective). In the far right corner of my tank, floating at the surface is a cluster of dead and distended tetras that, as fate intended, were suffocated by deadly chemicals. How noble to die for those you have never met? *Dulce et decorum est...*

---

[52] He is unemployed.

# Chapter 6

*"They were gone, and the lights of the towns and villages glittered in silence."*

*-D.H. Lawrence*

## In the Black

"STILL reading *Gatsby*, I see."

"Rereading it, actually. Just put the damn sticker on, Char."

"You've been *re*reading it for five months."

"It's called Stunt Reading. It's an extremely complicated... It's a tedious scheme... visual and linguistic acrobatics. You wouldn't understand. And your parents would still prefer you as a wet spot. Sticker. Now."

"It's not even two hundred pages long, Shawn. Finish the book."

"Do your job, Stickerbitch."

"Here." She slapped the round yellow sticker across the artist's rendition of West Egg.

"Thank you," I mumbled and traipsed away.

"Fuck off, Shawn."

"Whatever."

THE BOOKSTORE grows wild and bad-tempered in the weeks before Christmas. Each day as I walk from the employee entrance, through the horde, to the break area to begin my shift, I relate deeper to Conrad's aesthetic experience that inspired him to write *The Heart of Darkness*: The shrieks, the unsteadiness, the stomach-tightening anxiety, the threat of fatal arrows being launched without notice from the bush.

The security alarm screams, one customer begs an unseen coworker to produce a copy of *Hop on Pop* on tape[53], and four filthy children scamper across my shoes, rushing to hide behind a giant yet life-sized cardboard cut-out of a turtlenecked and leather-jacketed John Walsh as I amble between Poetry and Occult with my eyes on the carpet.

This time of year, the percentage of illiterate customers skyrockets to, in my estimation, roughly seventy. The percentage of employees who, despite each of our thirty-five thousand square feet containing at least one pathetic patron[54], actually *work* while on the job plummets to around twelve. I am among the greater eighty-eight.

The laziest of all my peers is Phil[55], who can be found almost literally any time posted against the wall in the break area spinning his day's yarn to employees dining from compartmentalized plastic. Plastic forks circle from their over-heated, whipped food to their mouths, but their eyes never leave Phil.

Quite impressively, Phil has not adjusted his lethargic work ethic, even after a two week suspension for allegedly calling our V.P. "an abortion." Now in his third day back on the job, Phil – like me, an English major wearing the obligatory khakis and navy blue

---

[53] "What on What on What?"
"On tape?"
"OK. But What on What?"
*"Hop on Pop."*
"OK. But tape?"
"Yes. Tape."
"You mean CD?"
"No. Pop. *Hop on Pop* on tape."
"We don't carry tapes. No one... Am I on Punk'd?"
"Yes. OK. Jesus! What about something else."
"You throw the ball to Who?"
"Naturally."
[54] Darn you, Uncle!
[55] "Generally one feels like his is an attitude like that of Shakespeare in his comedies: the world is an absurd mess, you cannot blame me if in our enchanted wood there are two men called Jacques." (Faulks, Sebastian, in the introduction to *Loving/Living/Party Going;* Green, Henry (Vintage, 2005) p. 10.)

Oxford – wipes sleep from his left eye as he enchants the minimum wage crowd with his

pompous anecdotes:

"So I'm walking through the courtyard of Trinity – I mean, feet from the Book of

Kells, right? – when I see this couple staring, just awe-struck, obediently, at a small

Wellingtonia. I think to myself, I'm like, 'That must be the spot where Swift started his

fires.' Or where Beckett wrote:

*Spend the years of learning squandering*

*Courage for the years of wandering*

*Through a world politely turning*

*From the loutishness of learning.*[56]

...or something, you know? Something, I thought. But walking another ten feet or so, my

field of vision was not longer obscured by the clump of portly American tourists, and the

object of the couple's gaze was revealed to me! It was their leashed and defecating dog!

A Cairn, I think. Shitting. This, of course, did nothing to disprove my Beckett and Swift

theories."

I jammed my corned-beef-sandwich-and-chips-and-pudding-toting brown bag

into the communal refrigerator, just between two brown bags[57], and retorted, pissed:

"Swift never started fires in the Trinity courtyard. He lit his dorm flat after being scolded

by a professor."

---

[56] I know this one. "Gnome" was published in Dublin Magazine in 1934, not long after Beckett resigned as a lecturer at Trinity. I knew that one.
[57] Mine featured a two inch rip down one side, where the sharp fin of my potato chip bag had sliced through.

"*Au contraire*, Jack! Dean Swift started fires in the courtyard at night, where he and other great and disillusioned minds drank spirits and shouted lyrics at the tops of their voices! That's where the Skibbereen came from, you know. From the dean's fires."

That was the last straw. I turned to Phil, finally square on but still without eye contact, and shouted through a clenched jaw, "Phil, you fuck! The Skibbereen wasn't developed until after the potato famines of the 1840s. The poems are supposed are *about* famine and flight for Christ's sake! *And that's another reason why I left old Skibbereen!*" I sang sarcastically.

"Whatever, Jack. Don't hate me because your preliterate ass wouldn't know Dante from Dan Brown," Phil retorted, paring a fingernail.

I slammed the refrigerator door, startling the four or five dinner theater spectators. Then, mimicking Char, I told Phil to fuck off as I marched toward my catalog of shipment ISBNs, banging my knee against the door jamb on the way out.

"Whatever. Shook."

There is no worse type than a man with an English degree who doesn't regret his choice of major.

I HAVEN'T looked Phil in the eye in nearly a year. In late December, just after the last Christmas rush – the stress had gotten to us – a men's room discussion about short story titles turned violent. I knocked one of Phil's molars out of his head with a soap dispenser. We're both still waiting for the other to apologize.

That afternoon, both Phil and I were lurched over our respective sinks, sticking our faces into the same mirror, stretching our eyelids open and swiveling our heads, inspecting our faces simultaneously for signs of very different but concurrent hangovers. Over the sounds of running water, Phil and I, by way of the mirror[58] began talking about our favorite short story titles.

"You can't beat Carver's, Jack. So subtle. So filthy. He's a quiet beast, man."

"Filthy? What's filthy about Carver? He's pure: love and booze and nourishment and that's it," I replied, soaping up my wrists.

"Oh, come on, Jack! Don't be such a prude. Pay attention to his titles. They're like the titles of soft porn clips: 'Popular Mechanics', 'They're Not Your Husband', 'Neighbors', 'The Student's Wife'. Come on. Don't.... Just don't, Shook."

"You're a sick fuck, Phil," I snarled at his crooked reflection. "Really sick. I'm prude, you're prurient." Impressed with my own vocabulary under the still-boozy circumstances, I provided evidence: "Carver is the guy who wrote 'Cathedral', 'A Small Good Thing', 'Why Don't You Dance?', and on and on. A pervert!"

"The best short stories," Phil announced, flailing his still wet hands about, splashing both me and his reflection, "have dirty titles, porno names. I could list them for days, Shook! Literally! How about (he began the inventory that would cost his parents thousands in dental bills):

"Agnes of Iowa"

"Obedience School"

"Dancing With the One-Armed Gal"

"Rocket Man"

"Plowing the Secondaries"

---

[58] Those very awkward conversations where each faces seems slightly contorted—maybe a right eye lower on the face than when not reflected, maybe the left—but all refuse to comment on this new perspective. All carry on until ending the conversation with a dropped head and a paper towel tossed into the bin.

"Mr. Good"

"Slut Wisdom"

—*Are you with me Shook? Are you following me?*

"Thirteen One-night Stands"

"Night School"

"The Potato Gun"

"Youth on Mars"

"To Do List—Week of March 14"

"Paper Swallows"

*My blood bubbled. My chest heaved and teeth ground against one another as he*

*continued shouting at the top of his lungs:*

"Ed Got a Job"

"The Price of a Haircut"

"Sharon Calls"

"Titties"

"Grocery Store Violation"

—*And last but not least, Jack!*

*With this, I clutched the soap dispenser fastened to the perfect white tile. My clean hand*

*gripped and couldn't slip away. I felt my fingernails peeling back.*

—"Lass" *you uninformed and ill-bred son of a bitch!* "Lass"

Silence.

—"Lass", *boy.* Phil concluded by violently tossing damp nothing against the wall, a sort

of slap at air.

With that, I snapped the soap dispenser from the wall and brought it down against Phil's head. When it struck his cheek and ear I was sure I had killed him. I was sure I had caved in his skull. I hadn't. The grey, shoebox-sized weapon cracked into three jagged segments when it connected with Phil's face. One remained in my bleeding hand. Two spun clockwise on the floor beside Phil, who was also bleeding. Soap was everywhere. Our bloods were mingling with the antibacterial liquid and tiny water puddles that had been pushed off the sink counter onto the floor. This resultant cocktail was a spectacular purple.

Phil was struggling to open his mouth, fish-flipping with his back against tile and his ass clammy. I walked out of the men's room, still holding plastic.

Phil lost the tooth and got a few stitches inside his mouth. His parents paid for the work. He didn't ask me for a dime, nor did he report me to bookstore management. Too embarrassed, I guess.

I concocted a story that had something to do with a menstrual cycle when I reported the mess to the cleaning crew. The oddity of someone having a period in the men's bathroom never occurred to them.

He and I – never close, but certainly friendly – neither spoke nor stepped into either's ten-foot sales space until after the following Bastille Day. And even that was accidental (his mistake, not mine). We have spoken several times since, always on unfriendly terms – usually me mumbling objections while he's holding court in the break area. Phil's Mac Flecknoe to my Dryden.

# Willy Eats Jack Smith

I BLOW three small but visible cigarette ashes from my navy shoulder as I walk back to the bargain section, wheeling several dozen paperback copies of *Between the Acts, Black Water,* and *At Melville's Tomb.* Today, Char says, I am in charge of stocking and sorting. My only communication will be with ISBNs, cardboard, box cutters, and dollies. I prefer ISBNs to most customers. The former are never replicated. Each of the latter, while occasionally cute, are trained by our Sunday newspaper advertisements to ask, apishly, about Harry Potter[59] and chai.

I also prefer boxes to customers. It is fun to cut them up, empty them, and throw them in the dumpster.[60]

Plus, on stock days I don't have to worry about my ten-foot circle. A customer could – would never, would not ever, but hypothetically *could* – approach me and ask where, Sir, could she find – excuse me? Hello? – "All Souls' Night" by someone named Willy Eats? I could lean against my dolly, which is plump with coffee table Canalettos, and, holding a copy of His Majesty's Complete Works, recite, mockingly:

> *He had much industry at setting out,*
>
> *Much boisterous courage, before loneliness*
>
> *Had driven him crazed;*
>
> *For meditations upon unknown thought*
>
> *Make human intercourse grow less and less;*
>
> *They are neither paid nor praised.*
>
> *but he'd object to the host,*

---

[59] At least I don't have to stock that big bastard.
[60] Intentionally ambiguous use of pronouns.

*The glass because my glass;*

*A ghost-lover he was*

*And may have grown more arrogant being a ghost.*[61]

"Sorry, ma'am never heard of him. But we do have some fresh and delicious cinnamon nut scones at the café. Are you a fan of The Arctic Monkeys? Their new DVD, *Live in Sussex*, is richly edited and to die for." I could say that.

No need to cast a third recommend. I am Stocker today. I imagine brazenly returning to my read, legs crossed, upright, chewing gum like a pig.

It is not Willy I read while resting – letting my tiny paper cuts heal – but the year's new *Book of Famous Quotations*. My favorite. I await it. Flipping to the "Writers" chapter, I discover that: Stanley Fish said that the act of writing makes use of grief as it might make use of anything. Reviewer Helen Vendler wrote that Paul Muldoon turns every poet he critiques into some version of himself. Jack Smith said he'd rather be caught robbing a bank than stealing so much as a two-word phrase from another writer. (*But which Jack Smith? Jack Smith the soap opera writer? Jack Smith the failed minor league baseball player? Jack Smith the Canadian politician? Jack Smith the English football player born in 1927? Jack Smith the English football player born in 1956? Jack Smith the columnist? Jack Smith the internet guru? Jack Smith the songwriter of "Whispering" or Jack Smith the songwriter of "Whistling"? Jack Smith the filmmaker? Jack Smith of NASCAR fame? Or Jack Smith of SAAQ fame? The Jack Smith who writes about fighter planes? The Jack Smith who, with a partner, snaps aerial photos of major U.S. cities, assigns a month to each image and packages them as calendars? The expert-*

---

[61] Though, in my daydream, the lyrics were regurgitated from memory, I must, in transferring this Vision to paper, inform you that the above stanza is the creation of William Butler Yeats (All Souls' Night is public domain poetry).

*on-human-metabolism-Jack Smith? Or is it the Jack Smith who kidnapped that little girl in Rochester last year? Maybe the Jack Smith who runs that billiards bar in Nordeast. Certainly it is the Jack Smith who is committed to pure innovation, originality, and ingenuity.*) We have, Mr. Smith, only about a quarter million words[62] in our English language, all of which are comprised of the same twenty-six letters; there are a limited number of musical notes from which to choose, only a handful of dance moves that our bodies can manage. Neither words nor limbs nor notes can be blended to shades so finely as you contend, Mr. Smith.

Ralph Waldo Emerson said his best thoughts were stolen by the ancients. Benjamin Franklin said originality is the art of concealing your sources. Langdon Hammer said that getting to the point is not the point. Emily Dickinson said publication is the auction of the Mind of Man. Samuel Johnson said a man will turn over half a library to make one book.

Whatever.

"What are you doing, Shawn?"

"Nothing, Char. This book is ripped on page 36. I didn't do it."

"Whatever, Shook. Stack 'em and get out. We're closed and you missed the staff meeting. Show me your bag before you leave. Although I'm sure *Gatsby* hasn't budged."

---

[62] That is, there are about that many entries in the OED. But, more accurately—though I would never tell this to Mr. Smith—how is a word defined? How can we be sure that this or that new jumble of letters means nothing, that is, does not symbolize anything, to anyone?

# Chapter 7

*"If you only followed the parables you yourself would become parables and with that rid of all*

*your daily cares. Another said: I bet that is also a parable. The first said: You have won."*

*-Franz Kafka*

## Symptoms

THE BUS ride home was uneventful save the mouthful of whiskey I spat on the neck of
the passenger in front of me. I was rushing it. There were too many swigs too quickly.
My gag reflex shoved me to a halt. She barely noticed anyway. She just shivered and
closed her window.

In my hallway, fumbling with my keys and squinting to protect my eyes from the
smoke trailing the cigarette that bounced at the corner of my mouth, I began singing
*Georgia on My Mind*[63], swerving, drunken foot in front of foot. Wrestling with carpet,
recalling the wind that pushed leaves in a circle around Peavy Plaza as Elizabeth and I
smoked found cigarettes and peeled through a stack of receipts; I heard the world being
crumpled.

I spat my liquor and love; blood from the many times I've been murdered,
grabbed, lost, slit, hanged, denied, washed and worn, and I just leaked until everything
was gone. *Marrow isn't doing its job, my pet. MypetMypet... My petechiae are glowing.*

Lazy mouth, red and agape. My eyes bounced up and I spun, unbalanced to
watch.

I saw my reflection in the fluorescent tubes: Millions of dollars worth of diamond
dents on my chest from snow angeling on a chain-link fence.

---

[63] Not the song but the entire album. Or so a neighbor later told me.

But the right key let me in and home composes me. Noodles and bacon bits and chopsticks. Beer and Sam and Ellis and Them. My balance was (is?) back; I am sturdy as book stacks: Unmoving, fortified, and slanted. Seated finally, I followed the C-O-P-Y and began:


## School for Scoundrels

WHEN I left the school, I left in disgrace, and, in fact, was <u>permitted</u> to leave as I did solely on the condition that I hold my tongue. I was sworn to silence for ten years. Now that the stipulated time (and more) has elapsed and free me from my solemn vows, speak I must – if only to show those wicked rascals that their plan miscarried, and that I have not forgotten... If many readers can't forbear wagging their heads in bewilderment and disbelief, I'll understand. After all it is precisely the truth which is the most incredible.

I have called it the School for Scoundrels, but it had a different name. In accordance with the custom which prevailed then as now, the official title of the institution was so dignified and austerely conservative as to be in fact high-sounding: Alpine Institute for Civic Leadership. I say "official" title because I have no doubt that a secret connection existed between the government and this select conclave of gifted students and dedicated doctors of philosophy. Of proof on this point, I have none, but of conviction plenty; and that will have to suffice for the present.

The student body was recruited in a peculiar way from young men who, at the close of World War II, had just been discharged from the various branches of military service. It appears that all who were considered eligible for the special, experimental, instruction in store were sent to Fort Roper for the purpose of demobilization. In any case, in a tavern just off the military reservation the school officials were able to sign up as many guinea pigs as suited their purpose. There is no denying we all were persuaded; not impressed against the will in the heavy-handed manner which the British Admiralty used with American seamen in playing the overture to the War of 1812. The Alpine's offer sounded like a good one at the time: no tuition, no red tape, no Veteran's Administration. So we signed up.

I may have been gullible, but, if so, I did not lack company. Speaking for myself alone – for the sales theme doubtless varied according to the vulnerability of the victims—I was softened up, made receptive to the alleged advantages of the Shangri-La by flattery. The school's representative confided to me, with that unctuous regard for my welfare which was his trademark, that only those with phenomenal ratings in the military intelligence tests were being considered for this first class at the newly established academy. I had such a rating, he said. Besides, I was the right age, and hadn't yet been contaminated by attendance at any other college. I listened without skepticism. This well-dressed, self assured, soft-spoken man fifteen years my senior was so sure he had the answers to the vexing questions of my immediate future, my education, that it never occurred to me to question his beneficence.

I'll give the devil his due. There was no misrepresentation about the physical site of the school. Mr. Boyd was a little coy when I asked about the location of the school, saying "That's one of the things I can't tell you, Mr. Smith. I can say this much, though: It has a setting which rivals that of Shangri-Las. I judge from your record that you know a lot about mountain country, but I'm willing to wager you've never seen grandeur and splendor to compare with that you'll see at the School." Well, he was right about that. I have no kick coming on that score... I want to be fair –as fair as one in my circumstances

can be...Give or take a few brain cells and I'm as average as my neighbor... I'm human...

I was the only student who failed to be satisfied with the course of instruction.

There may have been others who were expelled as I was, and on similar terms. If so, it

happened after my departure. There is the possibility, too, that a few others were

skeptical of the value of the teachings but unwilling to throw in the sponge and say

farewell to what surely was one of the most luxurious educational set-ups in existence.

Perhaps we were guinea pigs, and no more, but we were just as well-fed, well-clothed

and well-sheltered as we were tail-less. Don't forget that.

To say that I wasn't satisfied with the instruction may be claiming credit which

really isn't due me. It wasn't that I fore-shadowed those foreign students of the present-

day who topple cabinets and ministries and who, while ranting and rioting on the streets,

still have the presence of mind for the delicate task of advising members of parliament

how to conduct the affairs of government. I was intellectually humble in the best

American tradition. I was well-disciplined up to a point... But, <u>have</u> it that I threw away

the opportunity; <u>have</u> it that I flunked out. Have it any way at all, but give me a chance to

<u>speak out</u>! That's all I ask. I have no wish to falsify the facts; or to vilify the character of

any person living or dead!!

...But I'm getting the cart before the horse... I'm sorry...There were exactly fifty

of us accepted for training—all discharges from Fort Roper. We went to our destination

in three chartered planes, those good old oxen of the post-war airplanes known as DC-3s;

but we went by night and we cruised so high we could see nothing. We travelled [sic] for

seven hours, which was very strange indeed because almost any point in the Rocky

Mountains certainly should have been within a maximum of three hours flying time from Fort Roper. To be sure, no one in position to know ever officially confirmed that the School was in the Rockies, but where else could it have been and still been in this country? Looking West one could see tier after tier of up-thrust humps outlined in purple haze. On the clear days of early fall as many as a dozen snow-streaked peaks were visible.

Whenever fifty young men are assembled together, someone will stand up in front and give a spiel and tell them he never in his life has seen fifty finer fellows in one place at one time. That's what we were told at the first formation after our arrival at the School. It was the Dean of Studies, the officer in charge of the curriculum and everything else, who greeted us and told us that. We had arrived at dawn, and the reception assembly was held that evening in an auditorium the size of one of those cozy convention halls the newer hotels have. In the meantime, we had slept, eaten, and inspected in a preliminary, incredulous, way the scenic and architectural magnificence which surrounded us.

We were overwhelmed by everything. The buildings, all three, were relatively small, but brand new and absolutely out of this world. In color, they were boldly black—of dark, polished stone. Their lines owed nothing to known styles, not even American Gothic. The effect, if not pleasing, nor graceful, nor liberating, was at least impressive, even against the grandiose backdrop of peaks and canyons. Inside the dormitory, the furniture and furnishings were of excellent quality, but, as in the case of even the best gentlemen's clubs, in neither good nor bad taste—simply impersonal, rich, blank. Yet, nothing screamed with shiny newness, as if that were the ultimate in decoration.

There was no indication in the size of the lay-out that more than one class would ever be there during the same term. The Dean of Studies told us in his speech that persons of our calibre were expected to complete the equivalent of a four-year college course in one year. There were, of course, to be no distractions: no life beyond the campus, no travel, no co-eds, no schedule of inter-collegiate sports. This information was pretty ominous: grim, forbidding, and foreboding – and not to me alone.

As it turned out, the fall months, September, October, November, passed very agreeably at the School, with little sense of strictness or tension. There was a minimum of friction among the students; and yet no hint of order imposed from above as in a military setting. Everything clicked off so smoothly, efficiently, and swiftly that I, in common with the rest, was congratulating myself on my good fortune in being picked for the party... So it went for those three months.

At one of the class assemblies, the professor in charge at the time read from a little slip handed him by the dean's secretary that Reginald Smith was requested to report to the office of the Dean of Studies. I took off at once. The professor nodded perfunctorily to signify my dismissal from the room. The dean's office in the administration-wing of the building was less than a block away. Through the glass partition, the dean noted my arrival in his reception room, which was empty at the moment, and he signaled me to come in.[64]

The dean – his name was Aaron Bradford, but he was always called the dean – greeted me without a smile and waved me to a chair. I returned the greeting in kind, trying to "size up" the situation. In common repute, the dean was as suave as a diplomat,

---

[64] Someone must have slandered Josef K. (Kafka, Franz, The Trial (Schocken, 1998) p. 3)

as righteous as a missionary, and as aggressive as a Tartar. I could well believe this student appraisal. Behind the immense, massive, splendid, dark desk, the dean tilted back in his leather chair and looked at me over fingertips pressed together into a steeple beneath his chin. He seemed to be seated in a higher chair or on a higher level than me. His eyes were blue—light blue, not to say icy blue.

"It didn't take you long to get here, Mr. Smith," he said. "Did you run?"

"No," I replied. "I walked."[65]

"You're out of breath," he said.

"It's the altitude, I suppose," I said.

"Do you have an idea what I want to talk to you about?" he asked.

"Is it some news?" I mumbled.

"Yes... Some bad news... some very bad news... for you and for us... for the School."

I waited for him to continue. For what seemed a long while he hesitated; at an impasse; uncertain of the right starting point. Then he looked at me sternly and proceeded. "No one has denounced you. No one at all. Nor do I have any accusation to make. All I want to do is announce an irrevocable decision of the Faculty Council. It's not just my decision. It's a group judgment and you may as well know the vote was unanimous." He looked at me to see if I understood, if I followed the drift of it, his remarks.

"What vote was that?" I asked. What the dean had just finished saying had caused every watch-wheel in my brain to spin at full speed in uncoordinated confusion, but I

---

[65] ...he realized at once that he shouldn't have spoken aloud, and that by doing so he had, in a sense, acknowledged the stranger's right to oversee his actions. (Kafka, p. 4)

could feel in my bones a single meaning as cold and numbing and saturating as a fog from an arctic sea.

"The vote for your expulsion." That's the way he put it, without mincing words, cutting it short, without going on right away to explain. I would have felt better if he had not told me in advance that the vote had been unanimous. Indeed, I had the feeling it hadn't been – that this very many couldn't be telling me the news so cruelly if he himself had been against me.

He showed no sign of going on. I had the impression he thought he had done his duty; conveyed the order for my exclusion; and that nothing remained to be done now but to inform me to have my belongings packed and be ready for the plane's departure at such and such and hour that evening. I just sat there... Had he told me "Be set to go at six," I probably wouldn't have questioned him but would have let it go at that. It was he, finally who figured a word of two of explanation might be in order.

"The School is as disappointed as you are," he said. "We know your record..." Here he tapped a file to signify the extent of his data. The French couldn't have had a thicker dossier on Dreyfus. "What I shall never understand," he said, lapsing from his impersonal reserve momentarily, "is how one who know as much of the anguish and agonies of war as you do could answer as you did that question whether World War II was the last and final war." This remark of the dean may seem odd now when the Cold War threatens, like a volcano, to burst into flame, no matter when, from some mysterious inner stress, but I understood what was meant. The great war to end wars had just been won, and it was the official doctrine of the School that the objectives of the victors had been achieved.

"No wonder you couldn't appreciate the solid truths and the serviceable ideals the School aims to impart!" Now, as the dean's diatribe was gaining momentum, he was striking a pose of self-righteous indignation such as, in 1940, the isolationist assumed when lecturing the internationalist, and vice versa. "The cornerstone, yes the entire foundation of American civilization, is the rule of law. And what kind of an answer did you give in Professor Hobbs' class?! A flippant plug for the alternative of the reign of love..." The dean frowned in the fashion of a lawyer browbeating a witness. "In this country, Mr. Smith, we have a separation of church and state and in this School we have no place for the frivolities of the feather-brained who would dilute the purity of the secular state and the single-mindedness of commercial activity with religious nonsense. In this day and age, life is too practical for pap!"

He paused to give his militant wisdom an opportunity to wash me off my feet like a tidal wave or to bowl me over as a well-directed ball scatters and shatters a flock of duck-pins. This gave me an opening. "It wasn't as serious as all that, Dean Bradford," I said. "I merely told Professor Hobbs, 'Curse on all laws but those which love has made![66]' It was just a poetic quotation. Nothing was further from my mind than to stain the purity of another's faith. I was speaking for myself alone. I had no wish to complain of the commercial creeds which dominate the business sections of newspapers which I never read."

"You defend one heresy with another," the dean retorted, "just as they all said you would at the Faculty Council. You taint whatever you touch, young man. And the pattern of your errors touches everything held dear at some point or other. You have no faith in continuance of peace because you despise the rule of law which alone can establish

[66] Allusion runs in the family. This is from Alexander Pope's "Eloisa to Abelard".

peace. Only the rule of law, backed by force, can save us from extermination by war. But law can do it. We must have faith in force—I mean law. Where there is no faith, the people perish."

He beat his desk with his fist, but not to overcome me with his arguments so much as to beat himself into submission. His eyes were closed and a smile played uncertainly on his lips as if, just this once, he were having difficulty bringing into focus a mystic vision of peace enforced by the sword. He looked at me closely for a minute to see if I, too, had caught a glimpse of the spiritual splendor he had been seeking to focus and to describe... I wondered if he were playing a game with me and with his colleagues on the Faculty Council. What a triumph for him if he should be able to announce my conversion to his way of thinking and to appeal to the Council to revoke its irrevocable decision and vote for my reinstatement!!

"Where is the Heavenly City, Mr. Smith?" I didn't know what he meant; I didn't know what to answer; I didn't know if he expected me to answer. Evidently the question was rhetorical, for he went on. "Not up, Mr. Smith; not up. That's the greatest mistake that students in the ordinary colleges make, but it's a mistake we can't tolerate here at the School. Don't look up; look down. The lowest common denominator is the holy grail. Emerson's oversoul is really underfoot." He was talking more to himself than to me and it was a matter of indifference to me what he meant for I knew my fate was sealed. No doubt, the dean would be willing to champion my cause to the Faculty Council as vehemently as he had just spelled out the standards of the Faculty Council to me. I was certain of that by then, but I was sure, too, that his terms were unconditional surrender; and I'd see him in hell first.

The dean saw how it was, but he had another bargain to propose. "You don't know where you are, do you?"

"I know up from down," I said.

"That's at least something," he admitted. "We are in the midst of a vast wilderness area," he said. "There are no reads and no trails. ~~To~~ An attempt to reach a settlement on foot, with Old Man Winter getting ready to close in on us, would verge on suicidal. Plane transportation can be arranged, as you know, but there is no other means of coming or going. Do you know what I'm getting at?"

"I'm listening," I said.

"I'll make a deal with you," he said. "If you keep mum for ten years about everything concerning the School and in particular about our conversation just now, you can leave by plane within twenty-four hours."

"I give you my word of honor."

"Thank you," he said, "but, of course, we'll have to have it in writing, for the record and for a contract, and tit-for-tat and the rule of law."

"I understand," I said, though I didn't really understand at all. But that was the way it was.

At times all this seems but yesterday and as near as the mountain I see from my living-room window, and at such times I shake my fist in rage and my throat dries, thickens, stiffens, and aches to hurl out curses that would shame a solider... Then again, it seems like an affair which took place in another country long, long ago; and I hold no rancor.

Off there, somewhere to the West – maybe somewhat South, maybe partly North – the School doubtless carries on – producing civil leaders, mayors, coordinators, proconsuls—oblivious of me and quite indifferent. So let it be. I like it better that way; unnoticed; left alone. I'll throw my lot with those who wear the humble hats...[67]

Ellis Worth[68]

WITH BACON on my lap and a noodle swinging from my lip, Sam read me the following bedtime story, which poured through my mind as sleep ploughed over me:

> *Yet here for ever, ever must I stay;*
>
> *Sad proof how well a lover can obey!*
>
> *Death, only death, can break the lasting chain;*
>
> *And here, ev'n then, shall my cold dust remain,*
>
> *Here all its frailties, all its flames resign,*
>
> *And wait till 'tis no sin to mix with thine.*

---

[67] Worth, Ellis, <u>School for Scoundrels</u> (Unpublished, 1961; printed with permission).
[68] My Great uncle's address was pecked beneath his name, followed by, in his messy scrawl, "Rewrite 9/1/61"

# Chapter 8

*"Less bricolage and more engineering, please."*

*-Matthew Beaumont*

## Finally, My Formidable Years

I WONDER what his wife felt, and saw, when Edward Sanos walked through the front door on return from his service in the European theater of World War II. I've never been able to empathize with women, but I can imagine myself sitting in that room in 1945. I envision him still wearing his crisp green, a duffle bag slung over his shoulder, smiling, waiting for his giggling children to rush forward, seeking a swing from Edward's limbs.

But this is all conjecture. For all I know, Edward could've been wearing shorts, a scowl, and fresh gin on his breath.

This was my uniform the night I came home to find my mother, who sat on my couch carrying news that my wife was dead. Elizabeth[69] had always been adventurous and dishonest, both in the cutest ways imaginable.

She was the girl who tried to steal my ashtray. We decided to share. She always gave me the little things I wanted. And I always wanted what she took from me.

I was not in love with Elizabeth when she asked to follow me back to the States after my student loans ran out. I agreed. We shared again because I needed. And my bruised curiosity spread to love on a July afternoon.

---

[69] The Best Man at my wedding told me, as I buttoned up my tuxedo, never to trust a woman named Elizabeth. Her very name, he purported, provided her with myriad alibis should she ever be unfaithful. "Never trust a woman with so many names," he told me. "She could sleep with one guy, tell him her name is Liz. Another guy, Beth. The next guy gets Ellie. You're just the guy with Elizabeth. Tuxedo or whatever."

After playing a round of frisbee golf, Elizabeth served two friends and me a plate of cheese and crackers and a pitcher of lemonade whose ingredients were fresh lemon juice, tap water, copious amounts of sugar, and Type A Positive blood.

I have recounted this episode in blue marker on the cabinet just above my kitchen sink:

*Her left hand shakes wet, cupped like a spider.*

*The right slices lemons.*

*All ten fingers smell sharp and clean*

*As the knife's tip parts flesh just above her knuckle.*

*Blue blood blushes on the cutting board.*

*Oxygen and lemon juice rush through veins,*

*Setting her on fire.*

*Pinching, cussing, cradling the wound in her mouth,*

*Sucking with eyes closed.*

*Tasting her tart life again.*

*The guests will finally drink her, too.*

*Conversing so intently, idly,*

*They don't notice the bandage that wasn't there when they arrived.*

*The one absorbing what now sits quietly inside them.*

Elizabeth never admitted to bleeding into our drinks. But I could taste her in my glass. I smiled every time I sipped. Her dark brown, almost black, hair was wrapped in a beige cloth that day. Her natural lips would have been pink in natural light. On several occasions they curled up to near her sharp, sharp cheekbones as she glanced to me. Once, she winked knowingly.

A year later, we were married in an outdoor ceremony near the eighteenth hole of a suburban Twin Cities golf course. We drank with old friends and new family and women danced in circles to ghastly music.

Elizabeth and I honeymooned over a long weekend in Big Fork: A small logging city an hour's drive south of the Canadian border. We didn't talk much during those four days, each of which consisted of at least four hours in my father's boat, fishing and swimming in the same bay. Trolling the inlet shore didn't take nearly as long as when I was a child. The water level had been dropping and weeds were advancing strongly from the shore. As a result, we could not see the berries on the trees from where we drifted. We could not see the eyeballs of the cardinals, the veins of the leaves, or where the squirrels skittered. Neither Elizabeth nor I could see the details as we shouted, alternately, "Weed! Reel it in."

Each day consisted of one hour watching *The Price is Right*; and another two attempting to watch golf through fuzzy reception as we drank highballs and snacked on cake. We made love on three of the four nights: The last we closed by cleaning fish and depositing a white garbage bag soaked with heads, spines, and guts at the local dump before drinking ourselves under.[70]

---

[70] The man working at the dump was peculiar and stereotypical: filthy, overalled, and desperate. Driving to the landfill, I waved to him from the driver's seat. As I alighted the ride and grabbed the sack of guts from the trunk, the dump man rushed toward us bowlegged and violently asking, "How they bitin'?"
"What?" I responded.
"How they bitin'? Been fishin'?"
I responded, as our bag thudded into sharp-smelling pit, that indeed we had – at Brush Shanty.
"Oh, you need to get out on this one." He thumbed my head toward Antler Lake and proceeded to give me specific directions to locations on the lake where they were "bitin'." His torso was teetering from the hips, still giving bait advice when I drove away.

Elizabeth and I were silent the four-hour ride home. She slept from Nashwauk to Mora. The Twins lost 3-2 to the Tigers. It was to rain the next day in the cities the next day with a high of 73; clear on The Range topping out at 65. Another 15-song set comin' up.

Our honeymoon lie north, too near my eyes. A fat bee skipping rope in a blur. Sound is pitched up in Minnesota winters, but the trick is to dress warm, find an open trailer, and dream of these summers when that cargo wind needles. The trick is to wear dark clothes and stay alive.

OUR MARRIED lives were separate and pedestrian. I worked as an adjunct English composition instructor, teaching nights at a Saint Paul vocational school; Elizabeth was a nondescript employee at a Minneapolis bank. Our lives rarely intersected. The few hours we shared daily were spent on the couch watching that night's primetime lineup fold into the nightly news. Elizabeth invariably retired after the weather forecast. I stayed up to drink and entertain thoughts of pulling out a paper and pen to write. But pen never saw paper. I only began writing large words on my walls after she died.

Many weekends, I regret to tell you, Elizabeth and I spent apart. She often stayed home with family and friends as I, too routinely, fled to Big Fork. I fished through water or ice; it didn't matter. Despite our detachment, Elizabeth was always firm in my heart as I drank, fished, swam, and adjusted antennae in vain, alone in the woods.

The tile cabin floor was littered with sand, unidentifiable crumbs, and flies. These insects sat erect and wings up, either animated or dead. Neither coming or going, though.

---

He would have talked forever. The dirty man was lonely. I wish now that I would have let him spin dumpy yards, developed him, pulled in more of him. He would have made a great character in my story. Man could have written it for me.

EXACTLY eleven months after our marriage, I returned home from a fishing trip to find my mother on my couch. Her feet were up on the cushions. And, neck craned, she was staring up Beckett when I entered.

My wife had been drinking the previous evening. It had been raining. Riding shotgun in a friend's car, Elizabeth announced that she wanted to puddle jump, a routine activity among her circle of friends. Elizabeth unbuckled herself as the car splashed through a suburban residential area, about ten miles over the speed limit, my mother said the police had said. Elizabeth tied the seatbelt strap around her shins, leaned out the open passenger side window—only her legs were inside the car—and, from outside, ordered the driver to "Find the puddles! Find the puddles!"

Driver did. Elizabeth's friend told police that she had driven through several small pools at Elizabeth's behest before running a stop sign and broadsiding a state Department of Transportation van. After the t-bone, I was told, the car carrying Elizabeth skidded, its rear wheels swinging toward the DOT van. They met, abreast. She and steel collided again: This time the passenger side of the car out of which my wife was dangling slammed into the already crushed driver's side of the state vehicle, pressing Elizabeth between. Her mother identified the body only by a tattoo across the veiny inside of Elizabeth's left wrist that read:

*Tú que no puedes*

I HAD NO PART in organizing Elizabeth's funeral. I attended, yes. But offered no words. Accepted no condolences. I grieved. I did not celebrate life.

In the days following the interment, I wrote feverishly on my walls in waterproof markers. I lost my job as a result of my new hermetic routine and never thought once about money, which I then[71] viewed, along with everything that was not written across my fortification, as crude.

Some of my best work came out of this time (The Black Period, I know my landlord will call it when he discovers it!).

I'm sorry, Lenoir,

That I keep my car running when I visit you,

But I'm growing old.

I feel time is against me.

I promise we'll soon sit

And talk for a night.

For now,

I appreciate you staring,

As I espouse my gratitude

For all those times you kept me breathing.

Yes, I'll tell you I love you this time.

Before I go, Lenoir

I'll bend and soil my knees for you.

And push the fallen leaves

From your headstone

Because I have forgotten, my dear,

Exactly how long it's been.

---

[71] And still today.

I like that one, which is now hidden under my framed poster of Beckett.

The following is written in Elizabeth's lipstick across the screen of our television.

I enjoy this one, too.

> *It's lovely water falling down you*
> *It's lovely water falling down you*
> *It's lovely water falling down you*
> *It's lovely water falling down you*
> *It's lovely water falling down you*
> *It's lovely water falling down you*
> *It's lovely water falling down you*

Others you'll be shown later.

At least my walls are standing.


## That *Not Gone* Part

I VALUE my great uncle's stories for their anonymity, for their ability to remain unread for decades. No eyes viewed Ellis Worth's words prior to, during, or after the Cuban Missile Crisis. No hearts soaked in his ethics when Russia invaded Afghanistan, when the Challenger blew up, when Pac Man and Post-It notes were born, when Watts and Richard Pryor were burning, when Watergate and Vietnam and *Rabbit Redux* and the Atkins Diet (twice come and gone now) and *Watership Down* and waterbeds. Like their author, the stories were boxed and buried when Reagan asked Gorbachev to tear down a wall. When the Cold War, Ellis's muse, concluded at the outset of my teens, Worth's words, certainly not prophetic but words nonetheless, had been forgotten. Painted over but not gone.

That *not gone* part. That's what I admire.

Words can save you, maybe. Your own words. The words of others. Allusions. Samples. Originals. Paper. Wallpaper. Paint. Canvas. Brush. Tape. Mixed Tapes. Whatever. These can all hold you forever; for reasons I'm unsure of, these items and the evidence they hold are less expendable than humans.

At least they're duplicable – only slightly more than we are.

I am reproducible. I can be saved and stored and lost and saved like data. Elizabeth cannot. Elizabeth was never collected. I never even asked if she wanted to be.

Every time we watched a television show whose plot line included a character on life support, Elizabeth invariably was prompted to press mute at commercial and open a discussion about life support and what we both wanted should such a time arrive. She was adamant that, in the event she should grow into a vegetable, the plug be pulled. I always concurred and promised and snickered that I would pull her plug if she would pull mine. Commercial break over.

But death and life are not mutually exclusive.

*Would you want to be saved? Collected? Stored? Released like an album?*

She never answered the questions I never asked.

Again with Elizabeth's lipstick, I write – as I write, now, to you – the following on the large glass panel of my fish tank. Ellis follows the tube as it twists across its container, anticipating my words:

> *Dreams are pocked with shell blasts that feel distant.*
> *Curious noises amplified by near-sleep.*
> *Rumbles too loud to hear the supplications that accompany.*
> *I rest not sure of how much is fabricated.*

*As the sun rolls onto me,*

*I starve myself and walk freely again.*

*Relieved to hear the soft sounds of chains rattling.*

*Counting the walls.*

*Stepping long strides that stir up dust,*

*Making my throat dry. I can take no water.*

*The taste of nicotine is faint and satisfying on my mustache.*

*Like my shy-eyed woman.*

*Seductive, but I will take only Holy Air into my lungs.*

*I will eat and drink only His Word.*

*Praying pointed and clean.*

*When night comes I feast on rice and eggs,*

*Drink wine and light cigarettes.*

*The smoke, which I exhale in the dark, occasionally flashes yellow*

*As the missiles that steal my sleep take lives with full bellies*

Ellis would have liked that one. Had he known...

Staring at my final period and that ugly, fulfilling satisfaction, I raised and thrust my knee into the pane at the front of the tank, shattering it. Rolling water pushed variously sized shards of glass across my carpet and me, making us jagged, bloody, and wet. One segment sliced me across the left wrist. Another, long and thin like a ballpoint pen, stuck briefly into stomach, into my AT&T logo, before somersaulting into the water below. My socks, shoes, and pants, from the knees down, were saturated with varying liquids. I could not find my tetra, but the corpses of his mates were shoved into a neat pile beneath my TV.

Once bright, the dead are gray.

The ground was covered with splintered words.

*he sun ro*

*The smo    les that steal my sleep.*

*y-ey*

*ear the suppl*

*fabric*

*ar the soft soun*

*ke only Holy                ed by near-sle*

*ng pointed and.*

*D                    ne*

*y throat dry. I can t*

Lying down – pouring now from all holes on my ocean floor replete with life[72], death, and teeth – I felt the water level rising past my ears, now my mouth, and nose. The water folded over me as glass carved skin through clothing. The shards poked steadily and sincerely, like an orchestra's staccato-plucking strings. The waters were the swaying and steady horns. I, then, was Prokofiev awaiting the end of the rifle volleys so I can signal my downbeat. My audience sat silently.

---

[72] Somewhere?

Someone coughed.

The exchange was over and, for now, I told myself, I could breathe again.[73]


BOOKS WERE soaked. Water inundated stacks and crawled up, permeating page by

page, as if reading from the conclusions backward, toward the epigraph, toward the

heavens. *A Million Little Pieces*, wet; *The Wretched of the Earth*, wet; *The Cash Nexus*,

wet; *The Complete Works of Lewis Carroll*, wet through "Jabberwocky"; *Irish in*

*Minnesota*, dry; *The Book of I Ching*, dry save hexagram number thirty-four; *The*

*Autobiography of Malcolm X and The C.G. Jung Reader*, desiccated for now; *Dry*, yes.

My Concise Oxford English Dictionary was unscathed by the torrent. Gathering it

up, I opened to the marked[74] page.

> **Apocrypha** / pl. n. [treated as sing. or pl.]
>     **1 (the Apocrypha)** biblical or related writings
>     appended to the Old Testament in the Septuagint and
>     Vulgate versions, not forming part of the accepted
>     canon of Scripture. **2 (apocrypha)** writings or reports
>     not considered genuine.
> - Origin ME: from eccles. L. apocrypha (*scripta*) 'hidden
>     (writings)', from GK *apokruphos*, from *apokruptein*
>     'hide away'.
> **apocryphal** / adj. 1 (of a report) of doubtful
>     authenticity, although widely circulated as being true.
>     2 of or belonging to the Apocrypha.
> - DERIVATIVES **apocryphally** adv.[75]

---

[73] What is a *capricho*? A whim, a fantasy, a play of the imagination, a passing fancy—so say the dictionaries. The word derives from the unpredictable jumping and hopping of a young goat. Goya was by no means the first artist to call his work a *capricho*. Italian artists had their *capricci*, French ones had their *caprices*, and generally the word applied to architectural fantasies: Panini's assemblies of monuments, Hubert Robert's dramatized Roman ruins, and Piranesi's imaginary prisons (Goya owned several prints of the last). But sometimes it referred to dreamlike figures, in or out of costume, enacting their lighthearted or mysterious business... (Hughes, Robert, Goya (Alfred A. Knopf, 2003) pp. 179-180)

[74] Marked with a fast food napkin. I have taken, recently to reading the concise dictionary on my lunch breaks. My habit—unintentional though it is—is to use my lone leftover napkin as my bookmark. The following day, at lunch, I use my bookmark to wipe my mouth and the fresh napkin to mark my page. The same the subsequent day. And so on.

[75] Concise Oxford English Dictionary, Catherine Soanes and Angus Stevenson, eds. (Oxford University Press, 2004) pp. 60-61.

# Sometimes a Man Must Awake to Find That, Really, He Has No One

THE NUMBER Six bus took me to the riverfront. Jeff Buckley's *Lover, You Should've Come Over* had been repeating in my ears since my transfer. It's wasn't that cold. Thirty, maybe. Maybe freezing. More icy wind for the chill. I remember them on the big gibbet, just after Proctor was howling about losing his soul, keeping his name. They started with the old version: And he said unto them, When ye pray, say, Our Father which art in Heaven, Hallowed be thy name. Thy kingdom come. Thy will be done, as in Heaven, so in earth. But done before Amen. Ahhhhh men. She was never a witch, Goody Shook, but taken away and hanged trivial. No lawyers. Very prosaic. No questions or the wrong ones. Indefense. Straight to the gibbet to get that look. I guess I'd rather have my soul than my name. My blood than my skin. Preserved and not shed. In color and not text. My post-literate spirit. *Ar n-Athair a tha air nèamh, Gu naomhaichear d'ainm.*


THERE MUST be a dozen bridges – for feet, trains, traffic – that cross the Mississippi at and around downtown Minneapolis: The Hennepin Avenue Bridge with its monstrous Brain Melt neon sign facing west; BNSF Bridge, populated only by light trains and high teenagers; The Great Western and Northern Pacific bridges; the thick and sturdy Third Avenue Bridge, drawing automobiles north; the Tenth Avenue Bridge and its jogging co-eds; The 35W bridge and all for which it stands; and my favorite, the Stone Arch Bridge, which so many times has carried me from my favorite gyro shop to a baseball game, by way of water and the city's new theater that looks more like an avant-garde airport than an arts building.

The Stone Arch Bridge winds south and west across the screaming Mississippi, just downstream from the Upper Saint Anthony Falls lock and dam. Single dads and single moms trot out their dogs and children, all half bundled, on mild nights like this.

I trotted myself, soothed by the only winter water in Minnesota left free to move and shout. Leaning against the beige brick barrier, made blue by the theater's glare, I stared down at the water that will carry me south. Out of Minnesota, through Illinois, below the Mason-Dixon – maybe I'd reach New Orleans in time for Mardi Gras – and into the Gulf. After hitting that mouth, the path becomes the incalculable.

I got my Amen out and faintly, I heard a dog bark and at least one woman scream[76] as I flew, head over feet and back again, down. My mind was clean. My life did not flash before my eyes yet. I only felt a vague sense of pity for those hanging their heads and jaws over the viaduct above.

The water was so much colder than the air. So much harder than I had imagined. Some speculate that jumpers die of heart failure before the hit their destination. But this is only another myth of your living. Now under, I heard ghosts from the North scrape against the submerged branches and stray, dirty rocks. I thought of Willy's muscatel. I never tried it. Still tumbling head over feet, the impact caught up to me just as the rime dug violently inside.

Fluid popped through my brain. I had regained my balance and floated sweetly forward, face and hands down, like a superhero. The Mississippi wasn't so turgid. I could

---

[76] All sounds are pitched up slightly in Minnesota winters.

see. My hair flowed peacefully, sagaciously, like weeds comfortable with the sadistic current.

With my right hand, I called for the downbeat and, gradually, it arrived.

# Chapter 9

Epigraph & Eclogue

> *"Men killed, and died, because they were embarrassed not to."*
>
> *-Tim O'Brien*

## Constraints

IT'S ONLY the little things we choose. Free will, when you think about it, doesn't extend to many important things. We don't choose to be born. We don't choose when or with whom we fall in love. Sleep, hunger, breathing, and blood flow cannot be controlled. I never felt the desire to regulate, take responsibility, whatever. I just wanted to get and stay melted.

FOR ELEVEN days, a bothersome oak branch held me in the current, under the thin ice that covered the Mississippi at Red Wing. I never made it to Mardi Gras. Small areas of open water had developed as temperatures rose into the forties Christmas week. An antique shopper from Chicago saw my t-shirt bubbling and snapping in the wind as she took her lunch in the park on a mild afternoon.

She notified, I assume, the police who dug me out, identified me, and subsequently notified my parents who, too occupied to bother with my matters, subsequently notified Other Mom. Who subsequently notified Aunt Sis. Who wanted nothing to do with me in death.

I HAD stapled two papers to my apartment door before I locked it. One carried a childishly sketched and uncolored ghoul wearing what I thought were swimming goggles. He was smiling, offering his open hands, and had been violently scribbled over with orange and blue crayons as if someone was unhappy with his form. On the backside of this paper, hidden to the eyes of visitors, were the blue words, in Elizabeth's handwriting: *HE'S BEEN HAVING SEIZURES BECAUCES[77] OF DRINK* written over a few innocuous yellow and orange concentric circles.

The other paper, to the right of the ghost, held these words, typed:

> *To write is to produce a mark that will constitute a kind of machine that is in turn productive, that my future disappearance in principle will not prevent from functioning and from yielding, and yielding itself to, reading and rewriting.*

## The Price of the Ticket

IS IT WORTH trying to imagine Other Mom's horror upon entering my home, seeing the walls covered in words very different from those on the paper fastened to my door, but comprised of the same small bunch of letters? I know – that is, I hope – that the words stared at her with open jaws and eyes, legs akimbo. The first wall she read – that directly in her field of vision upon entering – featured numerous letters of roughly seven inches in height and three wide, read thus:

---

[77] She was drunk when she wrote it.

## nimhiú bia

*All this blood has distracted me from my purpose. I know I was to destroy you. But how? And why was that again? I know that your limbs have gone. But I just now have become aware that my eight fingers have penetrated the flesh at the small of your back and are embracing your spine. My thumbs cover your nipples. Am I to pull out? Wrench in either direction? Or am I to pause, reflect, and taste you in my hair? Why is this again? Your dead legs dangle, and your long toenails scrape my bare thigh. Where is my weapon? Why do I eat you over and again?*

Looking to her right, skipping the blinded window, Other Mom read the following message, built from letters of size similar to those above:

## iarraidh dhúnmharaithe

*Please gaze down my frock, between my breasts. I bow to accommodate. Please, now, see my bare and spoiled feet. Please be captivated. I beg of you, Sir, now watch my left foot slide back, disappearing beneath the silk you gave me. And now, please, be silent, as I dance you home. This is where the people pray you go, Sir.*

Still to the right, partially concealed behind my running television[78], Other Mom pushed her eyes to the next message. Her horror was beginning to subside, I think. She ripped the television off its stand, not hearing it crash to the linoleum, and read:

## maidin

*Such a lovely day! And this mourning! Is this a day to grieve? I should say not! Some say my dress is not black enough! I say this day is not! I say my dress is just right! When will this all be over? When may I change into jeans? When will my clothing match this day? When may I rid myself of this damned "delicate mantilla"?*

Pivoting her torso right without moving her feet, pausing to let the words soak in, Other Mom examined words to left of my kitchen cabinet – as closely, it seemed, as one examines a shopping list when struck by the feeling that something is missing from the cart:

## an giall

*"Shhhh... let me whisper this," he offered, digging his mandible into my shoulder. I knew him, I was sure, but could not see the face. As the man recounted his story, I measured the lines on his face, only catching this and that clipped sentence. In my mind, I saw the creases as they wrapped around his eyes and fell to his mouth.*

---

[78] A fat man with braids was on the television, uttering something about how W.C. Fields' bird of choice was the *chickadeeeeee*!

*I wondered if his tears flowed through these trenches. I felt his double chin bounce. His breath was sour.*

*"I looked for anything of beauty, either in his eyes or on his walls, but I found nothing," he mumbled. "Despite all this, I knew I was the ugly one. And the boss wanted me to make myself pretty like him." Then the man shrunk away. I heard the word "change" come from his crooked mouth as he backed away, and I began to listen.*

*"We were wondering if you might change."*

Now crying slightly, Other Mom looked around for more evidence – wanting to be convinced by these words.[79] She would never, I don't think, be so struck, but twirled about, once again to her right, now focusing on the refrigerator door:

## síochánaíocht

*Behind their eyes coffee and soup were being served and house music throbbed softly, assisting Cavanaugh in his winter mezmerization.*
*"241, 242, 243…." He pretended like he knew.*
   *"You can't do it, Cav. You're fooling yourself," his little friend chuckled, pointing at Cavanaugh, who, ignoring his partner, pointed at the snow. Cavanaugh snapped out of it around 274, figuring he had missed a few flakes along the way, and that he should really eat his soup before it was cold and read his paper before it was old. Balking at soup, Cavanaugh began listening to the*

---

[79] Little patch of yellow wall, with a sloping roof, little patch of yellow wall. I remember that bit.

*people in the next booth. A man was talking about piss on earth. How there*

*should be piss between the cultures in America, and, by God, we should strive for*

*piss, not war!*

*Sounded good. Cavanaugh decided to do his part. Shaking his head and*

*smirking sideways (pen still in mouth), Cavanaugh got up to go to the bathroom.*

*The men's room was empty. Both urinals were free and there were no feet*

*visible under the stall door. Shooting a quick laugh through his nose and mouth,*

*Cavanaugh unzipped and sprayed himself everywhere. He soaked the floor, the*

*wall, both urinals and the sink, clicking his pen with his tongue all the while. After*

*washing the urine off his hands, Cavanaugh left the john just as another man*

*walked in.*

*Without saying a word to his little friend, Cavanaugh grabbed his coat*

*and paper from the booth and quickly walked out the coffee shop door, hoping*

*he'd be halfway home before the girl behind the counter found out about his*

*experiment.*

*As dry flakes fell down his neck and neon lights bounced off his pen,*

*Cavanaugh wished he had saved some pee so he could write his name in the*

*snow. Maybe if my name were shorter, he thought. Like Bill, or Joe, or Al.*

Other Mom laughed, sniffed, and wiped a tear simultaneously. I knew she'd like that one.
"What else?" she asked either herself or me. Now with a wet grin, Other Mom peeked
around the refrigerator, finally to her left, and saw the another cluster of words, written in
a sprawling balloon, one by two feet, attached to the mouth of a crudely drawn elderly

woman. The character sits on something, hunched over her thighs with both hands covering her mouth, as if attempting to light a cigarette in a gale. Just to the right of the woman is the silhouette of what must be described as a goat's head. And still to the right is a faceless yet elegant girl sitting on a wooden chair with impeccable posture. Even without a mouth, Other Mom knew the girl was grinning at the goat. Which she was. These were the old woman's words:

## cé leis tú?

*My girl's face is weak. She has dimples where dimples shouldn't be: on her jaw line, under one cheekbone. The flesh of her face is pink sometimes, but slightly powdered. This is a girl who, when she grows into a woman, will not tan well. She has moles under her kindergarten clothes. Like a jazz singer, her nostrils flare and contract when she tells me about the dinosaurs her teacher told her about in school. In the winter, she smells like the purple flowers her mom kept on the windowsill last summer. But she doesn't listen to me anymore. It's funny. Everything you're taught, everything you are comes from the people around you. The people you love. They dent you and steal you and my baby girl. When those people die, everything you learned from them—and all of the lessons and imprints and stolen ghosts—floats about, carbonated. And you love them for it more than ever.*

Finishing this, Other Mom shook her head is disagreement. A drop of perspiration fell from her underarm. It was caught by her tucked blouse. She startled as the bead touched flesh and rolled under her belt, over her right hip. Other Mom cried overtly as she trudged across my still-damp petri dish carpet.

Looking right again, past the entrance, Other Mom viewed the next installment:

## oilithreachta

*YOU ARE NOW ENTERING A CONTROLLED AREA. ALL VISITORS ARE TO*

*REPORT TO SECURITY.*

*A faceless blue man with a white hat says:*

*SAFETY HELMETS MUST BE WORN.*

*A pair of boots—one blue, one white—tells us:*

*SAFETY FOOTWEAR MUST BE WORN.*

*A black-and-yellow exclamation mark warns:*

*HEAVY PLANT AND MACHINARY OPERATE ON THIS SITE*

*A silhouetted walking man has been circled and dashed away in red. He cautions:*

*UNAUTHORIZED ACCESS TO THIS SITE IS STRICTLY FORBIDDEN.*

*And then, oddly enough, a not dissimilar red circle and its diametrical line cancel*

*nothing[80]:*

*VEHICLES MUST NOT ENTER THIS SITE WITHOUT THE PERMISSION OF*

*THE CONSTRUCTION MANAGER. REVERSING MUST ONLY BE*

*UNDERTAKEN UNDER THE CONTROL OF A COMPETENT BANKSMAN.*

---

[80] A few plain observations, written in red marker, over a sign stolen off a construction trailer near the Little League field.

*The hoarding brings my train of pilgrims to a halt. Those toward the front of the once rapidly moving queue are forced to be repulsed by this un(fore)seen sign: Some point at the posting in accusatory frustration, others moan in fear. Those at the end of the line remain ignorant of the placard. They continue to push forward, provoked and foul. These opposing forces will surely turn our shrine-journey to self-butchery.*

## ONE END MUST STOP. THE OTHER MUSTN'T

I wrote these final words with such force that the effect was not composition but an engraving. This literal impression left little in the way of figurative impression on Other Mom, as I wished it had. On her or anyone at all. (Admittedly, it wasn't very good. But one cannot edit the writing on the wall – Pulitzer-worthy or rubbish.)

She simply read it. She never touched it, as I had once desired.

*"Brush your hands across the words! Feel the holes! Pick down the plaster!"* I would have shouted, arrogant.

Other Mom appeared weary, even sleepy from here. Wearing her plastic bonnet and windbreaker, Other Mom squished back and forth across my living room, stepping over landmines of glass splinters, books, and dead fish.

Other Mom was now crying as profusely as she was sweating. Liquids collected inside her clothing, which visibly grew heavier by the minute.

She slipped on the Spring 2006 edition of *The Irish Literary Supplement* as she approached my bedroom door. Other Mom crashed to floor, landing on her left hip and shoulder with a manly screech. Wincing but intact, her face teetering between an expression of youthful pain and ancient tolerance, Other Mom glanced up through my bedroom's open doorway and took in these words, scrawled just to the left of what was once my shuttered window:

## an pictiúr bréige

*Other Mom, pints in hand, led me to Aunt Sis and Sophie, who held a magnifying glass a pair of scissors, respectively. Upon sitting, Other Mom was given the embryonic makings of what will one day be Sophie's granddaughter's doll.*

*"Here's the doll. You couldn't bring pints, you chiseler?"*

*"It's lovely. It may be one day. And fuck off. You have a fresh beer in front of you, you chiseling little..."*

*"Stifle it, both of you," Aunt Sis chimed in. "Neither of you are wanting more alcohol. You either, Mister Designated Driver. You smell like my upper lip. And that doll is raggedy."*

*"It's not finished yet," Sophie defended. "And Annie likes them limp."*

*Instead of lobbing up the obvious retort, I grinned broadly and began staring at the barroom floor just beyond my left thigh. The linoleum was muddied and yellow, covered—for the most part—in peanut shells and grey purses. The scene could only be described as lunar.*

Squinting in confusion and pulling her chin toward her clammy and skewed bosom,[81] Other Mom read on:

---

[81] I'm no lip-reader, but I believe Other Mother muttered, "Who is Sophie?"

# maolaigh

*His eyes are blurry to me.*

*Like a Degas dancer's.*

*When he blinks,*

*She does so as a child.*

*Not a reflex,*

*But slow and orchestrated.*

*Manufacturing blows against me*

*I thought were not fated.*

*I can see strange fingerprints*

*Smeared across her brow.*

*My mother's clay-like flesh*

*Somewhere imbedded in another man's grooves.*

*Stray strands of her on me, where they shouldn't be.*

*On my neck, cheek, and mind soon followed.*

*Blood in my mouth,*

*Praying to be swallowed.*

Other Mom's left ear was suctioned to the floor. Her tears and sweat dribbled into the carpet. Had I the ability, I would have written, right then, on my bathroom mirror:

## in easpa

*She is a distant Virgin Mary in the doorway.*

*Sweating routines trapped in her ribcage.*

*Baby now knows the dark places*

*One can go when there is no love,*

*The same dark places she hated when they were mine.*

*And am I forgiven now that she, older,*

*Lays honest tears*

*Heavy on my shoulder?*


Other Mom rolled onto her right side and pushed herself, grunting, to her knees with both forearms. The left side of her body was dark with water. She paused on her knees momentarily as if in prayer. Then, rolling upright, Other Mom cocked her head around the right doorjamb. She saw this:


## cur le chéile

*Whence does the light come? It shows itself and now the words it illuminates! But I cannot see words from where I sit!*


And still to the right:

*They laugh at me when I pleasure myself. I laugh along.*

Over my bed:

> *Swerving, I walk the sidewalk glittering*
>
> *Buildings bubbling and eyes follow*
>
> *Foot in front of foot, smoke from my lungs blurs*
>
> *Veering behind me, footsteps blaring*

*Staring*

> *I know eventually I turn with no familiar sounds*
>
> *Or signs*
>
> *Trying to let their vision slide over me*
>
> *Shadowed, we turn right on 17<sup>th</sup>*
>
> *Heels clapping.*

*Thon*

> *Sidewalks don't glitter during the day*
>
> *I can wait until I'm alone so as not to seem lost.*

Other Mom entered my bedroom, craning her neck left to right in search of the few words not visible, viewable, from the hall. The surface that held her transformed abruptly from soft and moist to dry and hard: The hardwood floor of my bedroom was covered in dust and toenail clippings. There were no books.

To her left, Other Mom inspected my dresser closely. Its drawers contained the usual undergarments: Tightly bundled socks, wifebeaters, and boxers. Bottle caps, a beaded necklace, dozens of variously colored cigarette lighters, and a full ashtray were scattered across the oak top. The mirror that hung above my dresser was free of words. A wallet-sized photo of Elizabeth[82] was tucked into its plastic gold frame.

Other Mom turned again to her right, casting her eyes across those words she read from the hallway – choosing not to read closer. To the left of the – from her new perspective – left doorjamb, Other Mom discovered new words. She slowly sashayed over in order to frame herself directly in front of the, apparently and truthfully, hastily written cluster:

## an madra

*The Sybil, seeing that his neck is bristling*

*with snakes, throws him a honeyed cake of wheat*

*with drugs that bring on sleep. His triple mouths yawn*

*wide with rapid hunger as he clutches*

*the cake she cast. His giant back falls slack*

*along the ground; his bulk takes all the cave.*

*And when the beast is buried under sleep,*

*Aeneas gains the entrance swiftly, leaves*

*the riverbank from which no one returns.*

---

[82] Taken on the first day of seventh grade. Elizabeth had humongous bangs and obnoxious braces; she smiled recklessly. No makeup. No nothing.

I am assured, as Other Mom slumps to the bed and collapses from a seated to a fetal position, that this afternoon in my home – reading my words – has been a memorable one for her. She has finally begun to cry openly. She is sweating less.

Gradually, Other Mom's sobs dissolve into sporadic sniffles and sighs. Eventually, she evolves to sleep, snoring on my bed. The old love is curled up like a kitten with her forearm shielding her fluttering eyes from the light.

I am unsure if she understands.

"I understand," I said, though I didn't really understand at all. But that was the way it was.

Sleep disguises any agreement with my assertion: Life was an unblended medley of the tediously commonplace and the remarkable, with the former uncommonly outweighing the latter.

AND SCHOOL taught me nothing. It only gave me the knowledge to validate the suspicions I have had since birth: All things mingle pleasantly in death. I swear. The words, their letters, this sperm and that egg: I am the cells and the stories of others.

She doesn't remember right now. Surely she will.

# Appendix

Excursuses: The Uncollected Works of Shawn Shook

> *"He was very patient, generous and pitiful, to be accepted into their confidence without doubt."*
>
> -T.E. Lawrence, writing on the subject of C.M Doughty

SHAWN SHOOK was not an unusual writer. Sadly or not, he was of the most common breed: Of mildly exciting talent and vastly more unpublished than published. He was an inspired man, but his words – sometimes stirring, often not – went unread. And frequently, as with all writers, his stories went unfinished.

The following fragmented narratives were written by Shook subsequent to his graduation from the University of Minnesota in 1995 until his death in 2005. They are short so as never to be pilly. They are innovative yet, as Shook knew, derivative at times. And to what would surely be Shook's fury, they are now, upon his death, greatly immutable.

If it is possible for art to be exact, Shook's is. Like his still truncated and solipsistic writings featured in the previous pages of this book, Shook's words that follow are a spot-on representation of that life that he and most of us live: a long and quiet existence dotted all too infrequently by crises.[83]

-Brooks Doherty

---

[83] Sgríobhnóirí agus a gCuid Oibre: An Easba Misnigh atá orra?

## I. The Talk
(Unpublished, c. 1995)

*You're the one*
*who holds*
*my heart*

*gently,*
*completely,*
*safely,*
*sweetly...*

He glanced at me with a condescending lip pout and opened it.

*You're the one*
*who will hold my*
*heart*
*forever.*

"Awwww. That's sweet. And trite. And gag-reflex touching."

"Thank you. That one sold a half-million."

"I can see why," he cackled. "What else have you done? Anything else I might

know? Or may have picked up at a gas station on the way to my aunt's birthday party?"

"My best seller."

"OK. OK. I'm sorry," he doubled over, restraining laughter. "What else?"

"Here's one that's being considered for publication. *The Campus Perspective*."

> *To mourn me is to mourn the night*
> *Not to build a movement strong*
> *Many suns will be thrown o'erhead*
> *And the notes of the sweet lark*
> *Will make sharp his spreading song.*
>
> *To cry for me is to cry for day*
> *Not to summon deed despair*
> *Many tears will mingle with rain*
> *And the poet and the soldier*
> *Will into darkness wane.*

His laughter was like chewing. "You never cease to... This is... Wow! So

hackneyed!" One snickering burst caused him to spray spittle across my manuscript.

"Oooo! I'm sorry," he wiped himself off my words. "But you actually dropped the *v* for

an apostrophe. It's a pleasure to meet you, Mister Blake! My God, this is shit."

"Yet I'm gainfully employed."

"Yet you are. Yet you are. For now. Gimme more. Gimme more," he blew out the

last dregs of laughter and waved in replenishment, nodding.

"This was my first published card. It sold twenty-thousand for Father's Day '46.

The cover featured a photograph of a young Caucasian boy in a black suit, bowtie, and

top hat peering at the camera from around a pocked telephone pole.

"Awwww..." I was given another sarcastic lip.

He opened it. The card was blank. No message of love, hope, or filial piety.

"It's empty."

"Yes."

"Nothing."

"I figured I'd let the buyers compose their own messages."

"Why? That's stupid."

"It didn't sell well."

"Crap doesn't."

His amusement rolled into an apparent pensiveness. His shaking head was stilled and his grimace shrunk into pursed lips as he stared (I apologize in advance for this one, but) blankly at my card. I took this opportunity to quicken, suck in, and begin a diatribe against this foe that, given time, projected from my lungs and teeth like tiny spears. It started, however, as a slow drip, like white suds down my chin. Clumsily, I berated against his snobbish philistinism and coarse choice of words. Rhythmically, I stumbled across the most insulting adjectives and adverbs I was capable of offering. I was a lark, scattering my scornful song across the yard. My grammar was improper, too. I spoke of "me and her" – her being the photograph I gaze at each morning. Me being I. Eventually, as my wound was finally located, my tirade evolved into eloquent harmony, a communication between my self-abhorrence and his crassness. Between this birdie and that. I lapsed in and out of my languages: Irish and Latin, spoken until today, only in the hills of the Gaeltacht and the halls of the Vatican. I resorted to English only when regurgitating the support and encouragement I have received from my bosses and publication rejection letters. This linguistic shift – or maybe it was something else? – caused me to shake, subtly and circularly, like a bulbous bush in a slow wind. I told him I had to leave. No! He had to leave. That's what I meant. You must be, I'm sorry, but on your way. I envisioned him skipping like a lacy girl down the gravel drive, over and through the splitting mountains that only existed on my old horizon. His face looked like a crushed beverage can: Not offended, but irritated as if by a face-painted street jester asking cheerily for spare change. His chair squeaked and he left.

Just before the office door closed, Jacob mouthed words from across the table. He said, "I didn't like his tie." Or "I didn't like the sky." Or "I didn't like this guy." I was unsure which.

"Nor I," I huffed and never inquired further.[84]

I JUST THEN remembered that I had loaned Jacob the copy of *To Kill a Mockingbird* that I had purchased last year. I was overcome with embarrassment. The copy – particularly its first several pages – was replete with markings: Underlined words of whose definitions I was uncertain, sophomoric questions scratched into the thin margins ("How can we only fear fear itself? How is this possible?", "Why nap?", "How can a day seem longer than 24 hours? How is this possible?!?", and "Can collars wilt?"). I have grown so much. I am still not sold on the idea of metaphor, but as you may have gathered, I do enjoy a simile as a drunk enjoys his drink.

---

[84] The connection between the material above this footnote and the balance of "The Talk" is tenuous. It is the editor's opinion that the parts are entirely separate and were intended to be two stories as opposed to one. But as it is impossible to know the intentions of any author alive or dead, and since the stories were composed in direct adjacency, they are treated as one. (BD)

What must Jacob think of me? A grown and professional writer unable to grasp such things? Scout had been reading since she was born.

Jacob is passive aggressive. I am sure that, after returning *Mockingbird*, *The Satyricon*, *Ask the Dust*, and the rest of the load of my books on which he is sitting, the little goose will open a conversation whose lead question is peppered with words that I so ignorantly and innocently underlined throughout the novel's pages.

"So, these were great. Thanks again. Great. By the way, I went out last night. LoDo. What did you do? Very drunk. Very drunk. I was swaying down the sidewalk and this very ascetic-looking man leered salaciously at me. I thought him diffident, but I smirched lasciviously and shuffled camply away. What do you think? Did I handle it well? That is, like Gaius Pompeius Diogenes would have?" I envision him quizzing me – using his flaccid and hostile Socratic method – while picking at the Navy tattoo on his forearm that features a cartoonish boat anchor with his own name carved in a shapely manner where "Mom" is supposed to be.

Writers seem to be more narcissistic today than they were before the war. It seems the grand narratives of Life and Death and America and Communism and Christ and Food and Water and Words and Society are dead. Now we can only write about Me. The author inevitably finds himself inserted into the story. How sad for you, Reader. It seems half the self-deluded, two-sum (sum-of-two) trophied losers of my generation have grown through hot and cold to become writers – novels, poetry, television, radio, this paper and that pamphlet. Everything needs words today and everyone is prepared to provide them. I'm told theory – like the grand narrative – is dead. I think it's just retarded. Fiction today is only published if it's overly-indulgent, bildungsroman refuse. But the memoir is God.

Those snotty buggers who ignored math in the third grade – and were encouraged to do so – because they were "special" now populate the bestsellers list with stories of their pederast uncle, their drunk mother, their drunken Princeton twenties, or their doubts about God. They are rich. They are famous. They are. And I'm writing blank greeting cards. Or as Jacob calls them, "greeding cards." Son of a bitch.

## II. Planning
(Unpublished, c. 1998)

I SUPPOSE the plan was a tad silly, but I went along with it. My gums were bleeding that morning. Coffee hurt. My toothbrush raked. Ham stung.

"So do you mind? I mean, it's only one night," she queried.

I mumbled first in indecision, then in support, as I chewed my bloody toast and wiped crumbs off my lap. "That's fine. Yes. One night."

# III. Symbiosis and Embers
(Unpublished, c. 1999)

THE DRIVER turned a off the gravel road onto pavement, past a yellow fire hydrant planted around a crowd of yellower dandelions. The black Bentley skidded to a halt. I was told to remain still. The door opened with a "Sir." I fumbled with my notebooks and pencils as I came out of my crouch and exited. A tiny Japanese chin, spotted like a cow, greeted me solemnly; his pink tongue flowered under his nose. I stepped over its two-pound frame flinchless and strolled toward the noises.

Through the thin black iron gates, a crowd of no fewer than eleven dozen highly-dressed men and women hovered around a fire. The flames licked just above their heads, illuminating the spectral faces of those in the distance, silhouetting those in the foreground. White hand after white hand passed nearly empty glasses to a young woman, hair bobbed with eyes like olives, who blindly tossed the dregs of each goblet into the coals. The air smelled of smoke and burnt lime. The latter fragrance, so new to me, was sharp and exquisite, as I believe an early Rio morning carries. The coals hissed routinely and the resultant steam carried that odor of fried citrus and a touch of gin into me. Embers swirled and landed on the shoulders of the company. Before flaming out, they pulsed subtly and circularly, like a bulbous bush in a slow wind.

The woman was hurling, on average I believe, burnt booze offerings every forty-five seconds. Meantime, she held court around the flames telling the other guest tales of food: Why the Beef in the Midwest is Superior to That from the South. Why I Detest Mayonnaise. Why Milk and Crackers Go So Well Together. Why Those New Soft Candies Are So Heavenly.

As she regaled, she glanced at me and quickly glanced away violently, as if perplexed by an unexpectedly ringing bell. She crossed and uncrossed her skirted legs before twisting her bob to and fro out of a frustrating electric desire, presumably for a snack. I had to find Jacob. And someone was tugging at my sock.

At my foot, looking not dissimilar to an upright-walking Japanese chin, was a red-haired child in a blue plaid skirt, no more than three years of age. She was in need of something. In lieu of words or a hug, I slid my free hand into my notebook and pulled out a rough draft of what would be my next bestseller. I handed the card to the girl, who promptly grinned crookedly, turned her back to me, and opened it. I hunched down and dropped my chin onto her left shoulder. I read its contents and hummed a few bars:

*How can I be just your friend?*

*You want me to act like we've never kissed.*

*You want to forget, pretend we've never met.*

*And I've tried and I've tried, but I haven't yet.*

*You walk by, and I fall to pieces.*

*I fall to pieces.*

*Time only adds to the flame...*

By now, several guests were staring queasily at me. I straightened myself, brushed ashes off my shoulder and walked briskly toward a distant picnic table, leaving the kid unaided.

Several paces away, I turned and looked at my child. She had begun dancing from the waist down. Still grinning at the open card, her knees buckled sharply to the rhythm of memory.

*The way you used to do. Used to dooooo!*

JACOB WAS sitting at the picnic table flipping ice cubes about his otherwise empty glass, nodding absently to a vehement talker genuflecting at Jacob's feet. The talker poked Jacob's knee cap and spoke weakly of the past: "It's been a year since we met, but to me, only the first four months counted. I know you don't agree, but this is overdue. If the planes fly, I'm leaving Thursday."

JACOB WAS terribly young and gifted painter-cum-writer, one of those men who placed two fingers under the greasy foundation of the art world and transplanted it from Paris to New York in the 1950s. Still only twenty-four years old, Jacob had already written two autobiographies. Not memoirs, mind you. Jacob, I was told, thought the memoir crass and self-indulgent. The autobiography, however, was human science. It could be simultaneously hard and timorous. Memoir, according to Jacob was the literary equivalent to a fat boy with a gluttonous mouthful of pudding. The autobiography was like fresh lobster in Des Moines: So luxurious as to be of questionable authenticity. Still more opulent was the biography. It, said Jacob, in a note to me via his agent, "possesses all that is deluxe about that elephant autobiography yet carries with it that symbiotic bug-eating birdie of outside validation. Independence is all we have these days." And that definition of independence is what finds me here, dodging the smoke and children, looking for work.

Jacob did not greet me as I approached and placed my notebooks next to him on the picnic table. Instead, he kneed his vehement narrator in the upper lip, turned to me and began hurling thoughts at me.

"What do you think? Open *in media res* – at my first gallery show: Chelsea, 1954 – then flash back to childhood in Robbinsdale? Or introduce the reader to my death bed and then drag them back?"

The prime reason why Jacob, not long out of puberty, was so determined to chronicle his short existence as often and in as varying fashion as possible, is that he was convinced that he would not live to be thirty. He had had a dream, he said, at the age of six, which forecast his death of TB. His age was not made clear in this vision, but his dying body had looked "startlingly good, like that of a whore."

Jacob was slender with glossy black shoes that throbbed the bonfire's reflection. He carried a pink pastel shirt; he unremittingly wore pastel as a show of his bizarre loathing for albinism. His hair was thin. His pressed jeans just short enough to reveal a bruise above both ankle bones. "How about we start before the beginning?" Jacob proposed.

# IV. Flying in Sun

(Unpublished, c. 2000. *It is unclear whether "Flying in the Sun" was intended as a stand-alone short story or if it was an extension of "Symbiosis and Embers". This lipogram may have been the beginning "before the beginning" alluded to at the conclusion of "Symbiosis and Embers," with this story's unnamed narrator serving as Jacob's mother.*)

SLIGHT crouch and tight grin, a lady sits up, back against a pillow. His. A sun is big. A lady is, too. Now standing on floor, walking down and shaking from our morning. Almost dripping. That sink again. It's crap!

"I cannot brush a tooth!"

It's piss!

I'm damp finally.

Shirts and skirts are big and round to match our sun. Push away that iron bar holding us in. Grab my drink and stroll to a walk to a park to my folding chair. Watch kids. Watch growth. Animals scratch. Bark. Scratching bark. Plant. Run now.

So much is missing now. Who took my following?

1) Folding chair?

2) Food for birds?

3) Shadows?

Who, I ask? Has it all climbed into this sun? Did you want it all so badly? So hastily? Did you hold onto it all? Pawn my shit?

I saw my things last night.

Oh! My folding has chair come back! I sit.

I say I am sorry to you, baby.

Is our sun famous? All know him.

Nobody knows Jacob. But Jacob is famous.

Bright. Kind. Warm.

Jacob, today, is dull, kicking, and warm only thanks to yours.

But a big thanks to yours.

Is our sun famous? Must. Always punctual. Only dim for, probably, attacks by clouds. Sun do good. Always, sun, do good.


PICK MY birds to support with food. I toss crumbs at you who hop. It's hot today. You who twist around, sucking, walking as if us? How about no. No food for you.

Only sun and shadow for you.

Pat my stomach.

Fill yours.

Prod yours.

Toss it all.

My bag fills with you, sun. With it all:

1) Folding chair

2) Food for birds

3) Shadows

All our trains roll by, dropping hints to our backs, birdy. Growling and making your food – our food – jump off this ground. Catch it, sun! Catch it out of the air and swallow.

And you do.

I'll abandon my folding chair for you, full and rigid and a bit timorous, I know, as you fly over that horizon. Kicking and strolling.

I can suck my thumb, too. But I won't publicly. Wait until lunch.

All things click:

1) My foot on ground

2) My foot on ground

3) Train tracks holding bird claws clicks on tracks

4) Suck on dirty tooth

5) Animals run across bark

6) Stomach holding you – claws on stomach in I

7) Laugh, son. Always do good.

8) Lists of clicks that I finish

All birds fly in a dispatch. Usually that $v$ Commonly that letter $u$. What about $a$? No. Mold into a $z$. But yup. All birds soar across sky. All birds south to Chicago. Tripping onto a branch, all dropping solitary in a chipping unity prior to a following oscillation. Look at our falls from north. Dripping onto bark, sun. Snoop on what you do. Up my two stairs. Doorknob is filthy. Don't lick my hand. Wash both. Damn sink! I'm starving for carrots, alcohol, clot, sugar. I'll stay on the lemons. Just citrus this noon. How will I wash my cutting board? I must drink for us both, sun? But I must do so sanitarily. I must pay attention as I cut. I must look at my dirty hands slicing sharp skin, thick. I cannot track, sun, by the birds out our window, shooting south in a form of $n$. Now $k$. And finally $g$. I'm not to disappoint and I'm still thirsty.

# V. Exceptionality

(Unpublished, c. 2001)

SHE COMPLAINS that she never remembers her dreams. She says she laments the fact that she consistently loses large swaths of her consciousness, of her life. She says it's stress, I know it's the stress that's doing this.

I told her, "I had this dream last night where I was walking along the railroad tracks, staring at the walls of the honey factory. Someone had tagged *You are a Jewel* and *Please Adorn* and something else all over them. I was just walking and reading and walking and reading. And then I stopped walking. My foot got caught in the rail exchange. Metal tightened around my ankle. It was stuck. *I* was stuck. My ankle bone began vibrating. I looked up and saw a single yellow light shining on me. It was the locomotive's headlight. I looked back and the graffiti on the wall had changed to *Please Smile Please* and *For Beginners*. I turned my gaze back up the tracks. The train was upon me. I flinched. That's when I woke up."

Rather trite for a dream she said.

# VI. Untitled

(Unpublished, c. 2003)

HANNAH BOUGHT hard candy before our road trip. For each piece she ate, she threw one piece out her passenger side window, watching it splinter and chase in the rear view mirror. The cracking of cellophane was constant. One in the mouth. One to the asphalt. And so on.

"Because he was stapled to the chicken." mumbled Hannah as she thumbed a candy out the window as if flipping a coin. She subsequently giggled, as she does when uttering her cache of punch lines, the full and foul extent of which I have, to my great pleasure and frustration, been privy to over the years. I have never heard her jokes. Just their final provocations. My favorite is, "Get off me, Dad! You're crushing my smokes!"

Hannah sucked one of her props between her cheek and upper-left gum. "Stapled to the chicken?" She wrapped a sneer so far about her face that a worn end of her orange treat was bared. She was, and is, a nasally creature, often communicating via the olfactory mucosa, uvula, and soft palate. At her most articulate, Hannah is glottal.

The buzz of passed church bells snuck through the car window and into me. Hannah was nonplussed. She rolled two jawbreakers around in her calloused right hand like Chinese iron health balls and snorted.

"Why the long face?" Hannah offered, not to me but to her audience.

Hannah and I were traveling to the fireworks show in at Folsom Field. The sun was setting, crashing an outmoded blue into a fresh red, and the resulting jumble poured itself across the mountains.

I was speeding. We were late. But Hannah paid no attention to our velocity, only to its effect on her candies' vaulting off the pavement.

Hannah did not care for fireworks. She did not care for the way Americans celebrated Independence Day, especially in the midst of our Cold War. She believed, she told me, that we should stop sending our eyes to the sky every time something lit up. We should focus on our pockets, and on the hands that were rifling through them. "Thomas Jefferson said every generation should have a new revolution," she told me just after buying her sack of sweets. "He said that the tree of liberty should be refreshed with the blood of tyrants and patriots. That's what he said. He didn't say anything about hot dogs and sparklers and *bang, bang*." I agreed, but added that the fireworks would keep us from sleep tonight. We may as well make an event of being awake.

Despite our tardiness, we had surprisingly little trouble parking at the field. We walked a few hundred feet, first around cars, then blankets and baskets, then children, then a few obviously uncooked and grass-laden hot dogs that had fallen to the ground and were thus abandoned. Hannah and I found an open plot and let the air carry our blanket to the earth. The fireworks had not begun.

"It's getting late. And it looks like rain," Hannah moaned, having deposited her jaw breakers into her purse for now.

"We're fine on time," I responded. "And there is no trace of rain anywhere. Look around. The sky is a healthy hue." I glanced from shoulder to shoulder. That concoction that gives the mountains their purple aura just minutes ago had now seeped behind the rock and black was now falling. But it was a clean black. A translucent black. One that would not frighten even the most skittish child.

"It is so in a bad way!" Hannah shot back. "We should go. The rain is coming. I haven't a coat. And look at those clouds! They're ready to burst."

"You're sick. Burst? You're sick. There are but two, no! three clouds in the sky and they about as susceptible to bursting as I am. They're as ominous as your candies."

The ground sank briefly, accompanied by a dull thud. The first firework had been ignited and thrust through piping and into the sky. It's detonation was soft, followed by downward streaks of blue and red which accentuated a soft crackle. Several more of this variety followed, solitarily. Then, numerous devices were fired off simultaneous, their colors overlapping, causing the black sky to turn briefly beige.

"Lightning! You see? I told you it would storm. You Plastic Patriot! It's storming. I just felt a drop on my nose. Let's go." Hannah stood and attempted to tug the blanket from under my rear. I did not budge.

"That was not lightning, dear. That was the main attraction. That was a flash from the fireworks. Now sit down and enjoy the show. And that was not a rain drop on your nose. You have simply bedewed yourself with your own spittle. Yet another reason to keep your mouth shut."

Hannah ceased trying to reclaim our blanket. She stood, hands on hips, tongue extended, staring a hole through me as I craned my neck, partially out of avoidance and partially to see colors. I felt Hannah sit down. Also, I think I heard her remove her cellophane candy sack from her purse. Yellows and oranges twinkled toward the grass as the plastic baggie hissed.

That noise got to me. Muscles in my neck and shoulder contracted violently. I spun toward Hannah, who now carried sweets in her cheeks like an animal.

"You don't honestly believe that it will storm, do you?! You only see clouds and feel rain and conjure up these maelstroms because you want to leave! Because you want to go! You cannot tell me that you see these... these frightening clouds and... and these... these bolts!"

A white flash from an explosion veiled Hannah as she gently moved candy from her tongue to between her gum and left cheek. She wanted to speak. She looked into me wholly and softly, but only for a moment. Hannah then shifted her focus to the glimmering discontinuance above and spoke, not to me but to her audience.

"I do."

# VII. Number 845 "I Heard My Phone Buzz When I Died"

(Unpublished, c. 2005)

I heard my phone buzz when I died -
   The stillness from my desk
Ended by my cousin from Detroit
   Quaking keys and beer.

My thumb beside had pressed *ignore*,
   And voicemail was sure to come
For that last cell minute available
   Be preserved for the morrow.

I willed my vision: Point away
   from phone to you I
Could make digestible, - and then
   There interposed my phone,

With blue, uncertain, stumbling buzz,
   Between the drink and me;
And then the home screen lit, and said:
   *No message waits for thee*.

www.ingramcontent.com/pod-product-compliance
Lightning Source LLC
Chambersburg PA
CBHW020138180626
46810CB00004B/1621